Ballantine Books · Del Rey · Modern Library · One World · P...   ...ard

Rebecca Shapiro
Assistant Editor

October 6, 2009

Dear Reader,

Though it may not be wise to judge a book by its cover, I've often thought that the first line is fair game. And rarely have I read one so electrifying, so absolutely tantalizing, as Tracy Winn's: "Lucy Mattsen was nobody—like all the women I worked with—until the day the baby fell out the window." I knew from the first line that *Mrs. Somebody Somebody* was special and that Winn was a writer who we wanted on our list.

Tracy Winn's prose is absolutely stunning, and her use of it in *Mrs. Somebody Somebody* to weave ten incredible vignettes into a vibrant portrait of an American city over the course of the twentieth century is masterly. Though the stories all function independently, it is their interaction that makes this book so special.

Mrs. Somebody Somebody was published to universal acclaim in hardcover by Southern Methodist University Press last April. *People* magazine gave it a four-star review, and *The Boston Globe* called it "masterful," saying that "she has produced a book that will endure." We're hoping that with our paperback publication, endure it will, and we can't wait to bring this exciting debut to a much broader audience.

We are absolutely thrilled to be sharing *Mrs. Somebody Somebody* with you. I hope that you connect with it as strongly as I did—from the first sentence on—and that you'll help get the word out about this incredible new voice in literary fiction.

Yours,

Rebecca Shapiro

Mrs. Somebody Somebody

Mrs. Somebody Somebody
Stories

Fiction

TRACY WINN

Random House Trade Paperbacks
New York

2010 Random House Trade Paperback Edition

Copyright © 2009 by Tracy Winn
Reading group guide copyright © 2010 by Random House, Inc.

Published in the United States by Random House Trade Paperbacks, an imprint of The Random House Publishing Group, a division of Random House, Inc., New York.

RANDOM HOUSE TRADE PAPERBACKS and colophon are trademarks of Random House, Inc.
Random House Reader's Circle & Design is a registered trademark of Random House, Inc.

Originally published in hardcover in the United States by Southern Methodist University Press.

Some of the stories in this collection appeared first in slightly different form in the following publications: "Another Way to Make Cleopatra Cry" as "An Everyday," in *Alaska Quarterly Review*; "Copper Leaves Waving," in *The New Orleans Review*; "Glass Box" as "Glass Box, 1956," in *Alaska Quarterly Review*; "Cantogallo" as "Izabel Tiago," in *Passages North*; and "Smoke," in *Hayden's Ferry Review*.

Grateful acknowledgment is also made to the *Concord Journal*, Concord, Massachusetts, for permission to use the cartoon appearing in "Mrs. Somebody Somebody" and to Susy Pilgrim Walker for illustrations.

LIBRARY OF CONGRESS CATALOGING-IN-PUBLICATION DATA

Winn, Tracy, 1953–
   Mrs. Somebody Somebody: stories / Tracy Winn.
      p. cm.
   ISBN 978-0-8129-8145-2
   I. Title.
   PS3623.I6634M77 2009
   813'.6—dc22   2008049038

Printed in the United States of America

www.randomhousereaderscircle.com

9 8 7 6 5 4 3 2 1

For Nino and Louisa Rigali

Contents

Mrs. Somebody Somebody

Mrs. Somebody Somebody

Hub Hosiery Mill, 1947

LUCY MATTSEN WAS NOBODY—LIKE ALL THE WOMEN I WORKED WITH— until the day the baby fell out the window. It was break time at the mill. Us girls from Knitting leaned on the railing over the North Canal, airing out our armpits and sharing smokes. The baby was bare except for diapers. It fell like a bomb in the newsreels.

Where we were, the mill wall ran straight down to the water like a brick cliff, with the baby's apartment building doing the same on the other side. Lowell is like that with canals, one for every mill, dirty water running alongside the dirty streets, or under them. Nothing like those romantic canals in the posters for Holland, where flowers reflect in the water and there's a blue-eyed man behind every boat wheel.

Ever since lunch, a spring rain had fallen. Then a wind came up and the sun came out and glittered off the slate roofs on the neighboring blocks of company housing. That day Lowell looked good the way used-up brick towns can when the light's right. In the sparkle, the cockeyed look of the old buildings—how the shutters had peeled and loosened and fallen away—wasn't so noticeable. With everything shining, who cared if things didn't line up quite right anymore. The wet bricks and slate gleamed so hard under the blue sky you could ignore the sad look of fences missing pickets—how nothing had been fixed up for years. Weather had polished the WPA walkway. Beyond our cigarette smoke, the air looked as clean as if the smokestacks along the Merrimack River had held their breath.

We'd been talking about men. I was as man-crazy as a girl could be. I elbowed Katie O'Neill, the strapping redhead, and pointed at the maintenance man stacking wood pallets down in the side lot. "You like those knotty arms?"

She wrinkled her nose and said, "He's too short for my taste."

"You'll like him better when he bends over."

She said, "Naw, I don't care about his ass. I like men big. I got no use for the pretty little ones." She jutted her pale elbow onto the railing and sank her chin into her hand—a dreamy boozer leaning on a bar. "I like to have to reach to get my arms around a man's neck."

"They call that 'dancing cheek to tie-clip.'" Lucy Mattsen, the new girl with the Southern accent, chimed in.

I said, "Am I the only one who likes the shape of that fellow?" He tossed the pallets into a pile as if they weighed nothing more than playing cards.

Lucy scrunched up her face. She didn't have much going for her except her teeth, which were all hers and very white. She was a sad sack, but with a little makeup, I thought, she could have passed for pretty. She said, "He isn't my type at all."

Katie O'Neill said to Lucy, "I'd say you like your men in wheelchairs."

Lucy's face went red as meat. Mr. O'Connor, the floor boss, had her pushing him in his wheelchair between the bays of us knitters as if he couldn't manage. Lucy was floor girl in Knitting, which is where you started if you were like me and didn't have family at the mill to bring you in. She moved the trucks of bobbins along, hauled empty trucks to pick up the done jobs, and swept up the lint and clippings, which were everywhere, like the fur off some dark beast.

Katie said, "O'Connor can roll his own self around. He's got you thinking he's a vet or something and needs help, but blood sugar took his legs."

I was a knitter in O'Connor's room. He tried that stunt on every new girl, and Lucy was the very first to go for it without wanting special treatment in return. Wearing some cast-off brown sweater and lace-up shoes, she wheeled him and his ripe nose around the bays of that big room as if it was the least he could expect. She'd rest under the one working fan to cool herself. Her hair hung lopsided, bent up on one side, flat on the other—she slept on it wet, anyone could see. Someone said she was a nun who ran away.

Lucy said, "I don't like him, but I don't mind giving him a hand." Her words came out slow and round. She let a cigarette hang off her lower lip, trying to make her soft face look tough. She said, "Seems like if someone has no legs, no matter how he lost them, he could use a little help." Then she asked, "Who's got a light?"

I couldn't say as I knew any nuns who smoked. I pulled a pack of matches out of my apron pocket.

That's when we saw the baby. At first, it was like someone had thrown a whole chicken out the window on the other side of the canal. The body dropping there just couldn't be a baby. The splash it made was strangely satisfying. Something had been finished, sewn up, and you could say, *There, well, that's done with*. The window screen, which had twirled and twisted in the air, landed with a splash a little farther along. Next to me, Sophie Robicheau flung her hands up over her eyes. The baby bobbed up in the brown water, flailing, face down.

That open window just sat there in the sparkling wet brick wall, gaping like a dumb mouth, while we waited for someone to come.

Maria Sarzana—she was a mother—elbowed her way to the front of the platform and started to take off her apron. Maria's got a bum foot. I looked in the water. Rubber pants floating, the pale baby in them, bottom up. It had an air bubble in its dydees.

Until I saw Maria getting ready to go after him, it didn't cross my mind that we could do anything. I couldn't swim, but I said, "Maybe I should go."

Pulling at her shoe, Maria said, "Who are you fooling, Stella? You might break a nail."

Lucy'd already gotten over the railing by then. She hung on to it with one hand and ripped her shoes off with the other. She'd shed the sweater, and her arms—too thin and white—poked out of her work apron. Her big eyes found mine and didn't let go as she handed me her shoes and stepped out into the air, all business. She held her nose. Her hair, which had been hanging like spaniel ears, flew up. Two stories she fell, feet first—her apron flapping up in her face. Who knew if it was deep enough. I held tight to her shoes.

Katie O'Neill said, "Gaah," and leaned over, looking.

Lucy came out of the splash swimming as if she'd had lessons. My skin crawled with the idea of being in that water. She crossed the canal in six or seven strokes. We didn't cheer when she got to the baby, because we couldn't see if it was all right. She flipped it over and swam on her side, dragging it with the current, kicking like mad to keep it up.

All of Packing & Shipping rushed out and crowded farther along the edge of the canal, so when she climbed out, we couldn't see anything but the backs of a bunch of bent-over folks in aprons. No one made a sound— you could have heard a mouse piss on cotton. Lucy was doing something in the midst of them, on the ground. Since she'd jumped, each breath I'd breathed was one that the baby hadn't taken. My arms got to feeling icy; goose bumps came up over them and went away again. I hung on to Lucy's shoes. Sophie Robicheau began to sniffle and pray in French.

The man who'd had my attention straightening pallets sauntered out from the side lot to see what was going on. In the end, we'd all know his name and wish we didn't, but right then, standing by the others, he was just surprisingly short, not anything like what I'd thought.

A murmur started out there by Packing & Shipping. Lucy Mattsen had saved that baby. She and his air-trapping rubber pants. Noe Hathaway, the head fixer, a little walnut of a man, came out of the crowd carrying the baby under his arm like a sports trophy. The mill owner, Mr. William Burroughs, Jr., son of Hub Mills' founder, put his jacket around Lucy and led her inside by the arm.

In the doorway behind us, Mr. O'Connor clapped his hands, "That will be all, ladies." He let his voice slide on "lay-dees," so you'd do anything to shut him up.

Knitting is no work for anyone who needs variety. I watched the mouth of my machine—with its needles going up and down, around and around, casting the tube of one more black sock—and thanked that baby for giving us something different to think about.

Single girls like us lived in a rickety rooming house planted in the shadow of the mill, where now there's nothing but a parking lot. Lucy Mattsen and I were two of a half dozen girls at the mill who didn't live with their families. Our rooms lined up like stables along the upstairs hallways. The walls smelled like glue. You stayed there because you had to, or because, like me, you needed a stopgap. There was nothing homey about it: drab wallpaper, dented doors, and old iron beds.

My dream was to marry a good-looking man with enough money to set me up in my own shop. I wanted to run a beauty parlor. I hadn't come to Lowell to end up like Sophie Robicheau, slaving for the mill alongside her brothers and aunts and cousins, getting as used up as she was and no further ahead. The grandkids who brought her lunch every day would start in at the mill as soon as they were old enough to quit school. With her thinning hair and missing teeth, Sophie wasn't the only one who looked like life had punched her in the gut. Danuta Bukowski. Mary Karatelis. Nikola Georgeoulis. Corinne Girardot. I could go on.

Somehow, I'd had the wherewithal to get out of Granville, up in Vermont, where my father had been a quarry cutter. He spent his life in the belly of the hill, up to his knees in seep water, cutting Verde Antique marble, two- and four-ton blocks of it. Our house was smack up to a dirt road in front and the cliff of a spent quarry behind. I never knew my mother, and you'd think that all those years of keeping chickens and minding goats with no place to go but an outhouse would have got me ready for a life without niceties. Just the opposite. Soon as my father died, I quit my job at the wood paneling plant and headed for the city.

How a quarry cutter's daughter gets screwball ideas could be a whole other story. The happy accident—how my nose and eyes landed in a nice arrangement, how my lips came to be a fashionable shape—had a lot to do with it. People have always been pleased to look at my face and figure. Anywhere I've gotten, I've gotten because of my looks. But being a looker can make you think you might be something special. Let me tell you, you're not. You may have the finest eyes in the world, long dark lashes, lovely shape and color, but it's what those eyes see that counts. Mine were blind, blind.

Glamour and *LOOK* magazine showed me better ways to live. I loved those glossy pages of beautiful women, all those brides who looked like they knew the secrets I would learn. I never doubted that I could be one of them. Not for a second. Those days the world was my mirror. Nothing but shiny surfaces to give me back myself. Wherever I looked, there I was.

That night, when Lucy came for her shoes—"Stella? Stella, you home?"—I knew it was her by the accent. She was the only southerner at Hub Hosiery.

I opened the door saying how brave she was to jump into the canal, but she would have none of it. She came on in and crossed the creaky floor like she was going out the window herself.

"His daddy failed to apprehend that there'd been an accident."

To look at her, you wouldn't think she'd know to use words like that. Her hair bent out from her head at odd angles, and her pants hung long. She said, "I'm going over there to see that baby's all right."

She was barefooted and waving around a pair of the ugliest brown socks on earth. Her hands were more graceful than the rest of her, but she'd bitten the nails to the quick.

I'd been gussying up a hat, sewing fake cherries onto it and about to add a little veil. I handed her sturdy browns to her.

She said, "How could someone not notice his child is missing?" I didn't remember her being so loud, but I didn't smell liquor on her. "We'll just see what's what," she pronounced. I had to run down the stairs to keep up with her.

We crossed the WPA walkway over the canal, past Worsteds, where the air smelled toasted. We were lucky, working with cotton. The people who worked with wool shuffled through their mill gate at the end of a day, boiled and limp.

I asked, "Where did you learn to swim like that?"

"Back where I grew up."

"Where's that?" I asked, trying to see her face in the dark.

"Down South."

"Yes, but where?"

"You ever been to the South?"

"No."

"Then it won't matter to you, will it?"

On Suffolk Street, people sprawled on their stoops, enjoying the spring air. It was a quiet night. One lone kid skipped rope—*clickety-swish, clickety-swish*—in a circle of streetlight. You could feel in the air how tired everyone was.

Lucy didn't seem to notice. She clomped along next to me in those shoes. Even by streetlight, I could see her eyebrows were in need of a good shaping, but she had fine cheekbones.

That afternoon with Lucy gone, folks in Knitting had talked about her. Katie O'Neill had said it must be true Lucy was a nun, what with her self-sacrifice and all. And hadn't we seen the shoes she wore? Who but a nun?

Teresa Bukowski said that was no kind of proof. She'd heard Lucy was a debutante. We all laughed at that one, but she said, "No kidding. How else are you going to explain those teeth?"

Mr. O'Connor put an end to it all, saying, "She's really the Queen of Sheba. Get back to work."

Lucy hadn't told anyone her story. Marching down the street next to her, I asked, "How did you know what to do to make him breathe again?"

"Learning to swim and do first aid was part of growing up in my daddy's household."

"Why?"

"There was a pool where we lived."

The only pool I knew was one at the Chelmsford Arms. But that was for paying guests of the hotel.

She slowed down. "Let's try this one." She stepped into a vestibule that smelled of spices and rotting wood. By what little streetlight squeaked in, we looked for his name. Except she didn't know his name, exactly. She said the baby was Greek.

"That's all you know? We'll never find him." I ran my finger down the line of names, many more than there were floors. Almost all Greek. "Birds of a feather."

She said, "I just need to know that baby's really okay." Her lips started to tremble. I tried to tell her she should feel good. She'd done her part for that kid. The air went out of her. Her back sagged, and just like that, she was crying.

I wasn't good with crying women. My stepmother never quit sniffling, and I got out of there young.

Lucy sucked a ragged breath and blew her nose on a handkerchief she pulled out of her back pocket. I thought, if this were a man weeping, what would I do? Well, I'd find him a drink. She said she didn't want one. So we moseyed back the way we'd come.

The mill, with its windows lit, reflected in the smooth water of the canal like something grand in the movies, like a place Hollywood could feel nostalgic about.

As we walked, she said, "It isn't right for me to blame the baby's father. I know just the kind of tired he was. He's probably afraid he'll lose his job if he says no to unpaid overtime. He works whatever he's told to work, which is too much, probably night shifts, and then when it's his turn to watch the baby, he can't keep his eyes open." She used her hands. "The boy's next to him on the bed, and the window's open because the man can't afford a fan, and the baby is a bright little thing and wants to look out at the world. So he crawls across the bed and stands up. All he wants is to look out, just to get a gander at the life around him. He leans on the screen and that's all it takes." She stopped in the middle of the block and turned toward me. On that side of the street, everything but our boardinghouse was dark, and I couldn't see her well. "Since when is curiosity a luxury?" she asked.

It seemed to me that we didn't have it any better than the baby's father, or any worse. Millwork was millwork. "What can you do about it?" I said.

She opened our squeaky boardinghouse door and held it for me. "That's what I keep asking myself."

We parted at the top of the staircase, but afterward, I looked around my room—at the peeling paint of the wainscoting, the path worn in the old floor from the bed to the door, and the bed to the corner sink, and I thought, everything that happened in mill life had happened before, and would maybe happen again, with or without someone like Lucy trying to make it right.

For a long while I didn't pay much attention to Lucy for the simple reason that she wasn't a man. I didn't have girl friends, really. All of my waking thoughts went toward my next date. In those days, I had my sights on Bucky Thompson.

Bucky was one of those sandy-haired people who can't sit still for more than a minute because his energy fizzed up somewhere, in tapping fingers or a shifty seat. Bucky said he couldn't always go out, because he had his old mother to care for. We liked to double date with his buddy Pete Jenks.

Lucy seemed like a girl I'd never have to worry about losing boyfriends to, so I tried to get her to go out with us.

I said, "I know a fellow you might like."

"Do you like him?"

I shrugged, "Yeah, he's okay."

"Then why are you foisting him off on me?"

I said, "I just thought you'd like him."

"So there's something about him that's not good enough for you?"

"No, well, he's not really my type, but he's nice."

She put her hands on her hips. "Is there something wrong with the way he looks?"

"He has a big nose, but I thought you'd like him because he's sensitive. He keeps a diary."

She narrowed her eyes. "So you think he's a homo with a huge nose, which might be just about right for me?"

She'd come looking for me now and then to share a cigarette at break time. We started to fall in together, maybe because we were both outsiders. She brushed off anything I asked about herself or her life before she had come to Lowell with a million questions of her own. We'd be leaning on the splintery railing, staring down at the water she'd plunged into, and she'd look around to see that we were alone and then ask how long had Julia had that wheeze? Or had I noticed that Maria, the spinner, was going deaf?

There'd been a lot of union talk recently—a lot of whispering—and I wondered what she was getting at.

"Is it true Charlotte Stackley lost her hearing running that same spinning machine as Maria?" she asked.

I'd been there less than a year, but anyone knew a person could go deaf working in a mill. Noise bounced off the high ceilings. Downstairs, the cotton processing machines didn't let up, like drums strong enough to slant your heartbeat. Their *thump-thump* shook the building, reaching up through the floors to the Knitting room, where our rows of circular weave machines whirred like dentists' drills.

Charlotte Stackley was old and deaf, but because she did what she was told and kept her head down, management liked her. She hadn't been laid off; now she worked in the boarding room, shaping socks. Except for the sock stretchers down in back, which sounded like the drummer's whisk at the Colonnade Ballroom, the boarding room stayed pretty quiet, almost as if it had floated free of the bump and clack of the other floors—nothing but women's hands smoothing damp socks onto the foot molds, sliding dry ones off, women's hands sorting piles of limp soft socks, making pairs and repiling them by the dozen.

Lucy squinted her round eyes, and said, "Wasn't it just a little late to move Charlotte to a quiet place?"

"She's lucky to still have work." I flicked ashes toward the canal, where they disappeared before they hit the swirl of brown water.

She straightened out of her usual slouch and said, "That's just the attitude management hopes for, and exploits."

Exploits. Union talk coming right out of Lucy. I watched a cloud skidding away behind the chimneys of the baby's apartment building and said, "You've got to go along to get along. Otherwise, they'll show you right out the door." I handed her what was left of the cigarette we were sharing.

"How would you feel if Mr. William Burroughs decided to hire his retriever to run the Knitting room?" Mr. Burroughs owned the operation. She dropped the cigarette and stamped it out like she was mad at it.

"Might be an improvement over O'Connor," I laughed.

But there wasn't a hint of a smile anywhere on her face. Sure, the bosses had favorites, and some people worked overtime without overtime pay, but I couldn't see what difference a union would make. In those days, management had a saying: "You can squawk, but the door's as open as the shop." That was because of a new law that said mills could hire anyone they wanted, union or not. That was how I'd got my job. I didn't worry about working conditions because knitters who'd been there during the strikes before the war said things were nowhere near as bad as then. And O'Connor looked out for me. It took an occasional kiss on his cheek or sometimes a spell of sitting in his lap. He had a greasy scalp and dandruff all over his shoulders but was harmless enough.

I said, "Your fussing isn't going to get you anything but trouble."

Lucy straightened her shabby shirt collar. Our break was over. We joined the others. She passed through the door with the rest of us, but something more than just her Southern-ness made her different.

Lucy swept the floor with a broom as wide as she was tall, trudging after it and turning, trudging and turning, rounding up the lint and clippings that elsewise stuck to our clothes and hair—the picture of the put-upon worker, her shoulders stooped, her hair limp, no one you'd expect anything from. But then, as she passed me, she'd shift her eyes in O'Connor's direction—

waiting until I'd seen him crabbing his way along in his wheelchair—and say something like, "New land speed record holder making news." She was sly that way, not missing a trick and delivering her cockeyed commentary out the side of her mouth in a way that surprised me every time. By then, we'd gotten pretty comfortable with each other. She'd see me freshening up my lipstick and say, "Whenever Betty Boop is ready, there's a truckload of bobbins waiting for her."

I started to look forward to the entertaining ways she'd break the day's routine. One time, she brought a cigar for us to try, saying she wanted to see why men made such a big deal. We were both coughing and, as she said, bilious in no time, hanging on to the railing of the platform like landlubbers clinging to a heaving boat rail. The rest of the girls held their noses and laughed at us.

One day, she pinned a cartoon from the *Lowell Sun* onto my door. It was these two fellows:

I thought it was funny, but maybe not so funny that you'd want someone else to see it, so I marched across to her room. Maybe I only knocked as I was opening the door, I don't remember, but I surprised her. She jumped up, clapping shut some kind of ledger, which she stuffed into her bureau drawer, fast.

I said, "Sorry. Didn't mean to scare you." Her room was even worse than mine. A water stain ran from the ceiling all down the wall behind her, and someone long ago had drawn flowers springing up from the wainscoting in dark pencil. The sorry little space could have been anybody's.

She saw the cartoon in my hand and said, "I wanted to let you down easy. Maybe laughing." She held out a jar of licorice to me. Her tongue was as brown as her sweater. I shook my head. I didn't want to look like her.

"I know you're hell-bent to be Mrs. Somebody Somebody, but it's not going to be Mrs. Bucky Thompson," she said, taking a bite of licorice. "I overheard Pete Jenks telling O'Connor that Bucky Thompson's wife is a real dish."

I yanked out the bobby pins holding my hat. "That son of a bitch."

Mrs. Somebody Somebody was exactly who I wanted to be. The way some kids grow up knowing they want to be mayor, want to have their name in the book of history, I wanted to wear a white dress and a ring that said I was taken care of. It was all mixed up with my hankering to live better, to have pretty things, to be glamorous. I wanted that Mrs. title like it was what I was born for—a want that settles into you when you are very young and grows as you grow.

She scuffed toward me in her stocking feet, tilting her head like a dog, watching my face.

"How many dishes does one man need?" I asked, jerking my hat off. "His old mother needs him, my foot."

She took hold of my shoulders like she might hug me. Maybe she saw through my blustering and thought I was going to cry. Her turned-down eyes filled with understanding. I smoothed the veil on the hat I held between us. "You must think I'm dumb as a stump."

She held my cheeks in her hands, as if she was memorizing my face. Then she turned away. "Far from it." She plunked down in her chair. "I think he's a bounder who led you on," she said. "Your problem is you want to get married."

"Isn't that what we all want?" I tossed my hat onto the bed. "I should've known," I said. "When he first picked me up at Harley's Café, he ordered an 'Angel's Tit.' Who but a stinker would order *that* to drink?"

Lucy crossed her legs and said, "Men are simple people. I'm not sure that most of them think a whole lot."

I was supposed to chuckle, but I sat on her saggy bed and sagged right along with it. "At least you always know what they want."

"You tell them they can't have it, they try anyway." She rolled her eyes back in her head so the whites showed, and fluttered her eyelashes dramatically, horribly, like a blind person having a fit.

I couldn't help but laugh. But she grabbed my knees and fixed me with a look. "You're way too good for the likes of him, married or not."

> ### Angel's Tit Recipe
> *Ingredients: 1/4 oz white crème de cacao*
> *1/4 oz sloe gin*
> *1/4 oz brandy*
> *1/4 oz light cream*
> *Directions: Pour ingredients carefully, in order*
> *given, into a poussé café glass so that they*
> *do not mix.*

After work the next day, Katie O'Neill, Teresa Bukowski and her mother Danuta, Lucy, and I traipsed down Aiken Street over the Ouellette Bridge to cool off in the river. Walking was like swimming in soup, it was so humid. Five mill girls straggling down to the water: one giant redhead, pink in the face; a couple of bowlegged Polacks working hard to keep up with Katie; me, so hot I made no effort to hide the dark haloes around the armholes of my shift; and Lucy, who said it was just like a spring day in her hometown, hardly breaking a sweat at all, even in her slacks.

Bucky would be waiting for me at the Paramount in fifteen minutes. I was standing him up.

Lucy popped tar bubbles by the curb with a stick as we went along, the tar slumping back on itself like molasses. I stopped halfway across the bridge to light a cigarette. The river stretched below us. In the flat, white light of the day, I couldn't see the match flame until Lucy held her hands around it.

She said, "Now tell me honestly." She settled her eyes on me. "You don't miss Bucky one bit."

Bucky's Stella of the day before seemed like a sweet deluded relative I'd been close with once. The air between us and the "mile of mills" wavered. Hub Hosiery hunkered on the bank and beyond it: one mammoth flat-topped brick building after another; the Merrimack, the Massachusetts, the Boott, and their tons of smokestacks, row upon row of windows reflecting the afternoon sun—all of it wavering in the heat as if stone and brick and glass would melt in a minute.

I said, "He wasted my time," and handed her the cigarette. "He isn't the only bubble in the champagne glass."

"I wouldn't let you go so easily." She squinted at me.

"He'll get the message when I don't show up."

She looked at the pavement. "You make people love you, Stella."

"Too bad for him."

We followed the others down the bank through the scraggly bushes on the far side of the bridge. Katie, who had a Brownie camera with her, put it down on a rock, threw off her shoes, and plowed in. We slid our feet on the cool hard mud in the shadow of the bridge. Lucy rolled her slacks up to her knees.

Danuta and Teresa held hands and stepped in. Teresa squeaked. She was a softer version of her mother—short and round everywhere. Danuta kept her hair in the old style and had that wary way about her of people who had been cold and hungry in the bad times. Her hands were like knots. She'd been working at Hub since before the Depression, and her English wasn't too good. She splashed water on her face and didn't let go of her daughter.

When I felt the water, I wished I could swim. I rested my eyes on the empty shade under the arch of the bridge. Bucky hadn't been all that special. I'd been stupid, no bones about it. The rippling of the water echoed under the bridge—a comforting noise. I wished I had a bathing suit. I had the figure for it.

Lucy tucked her hair behind her ear and skipped a stone, making it spin and stutter away across the top of the water. She asked, "Aren't you going in?"

I looked at the water, and confessed, "I never learned."

She cocked her head at me. "You pulling my leg?"

"Nope."

"Come here, and I'll show you how to float."

"I'd sink like a stone."

"No, you won't." She sounded so sure. "You're going to lie down on the water." She took my hand and led me deeper in. "I'm not going to let you sink, but it's going to be the water that supports you."

"Sure, and then I'll rise up and walk on it."

"First, you have to relax." She put my arm around her neck. She lifted me. "If you get all stiff, it won't work."

I hung on to her neck while she lowered and laid me out on the water. Her eyes moved down the length of me while my dress soaked through. She looked so earnest, almost tender, that I wanted to laugh.

Katie whooped at the sight of us and turned her Brownie on us. "Stella doesn't know how to swim!"

At first, I was giggling too much. But then I saw how Teresa watched us and knew she didn't know how, either. Lucy cradled me, one arm under the backs of my legs and the other under my shoulders.

"Just call me Esther Williams," I said, my feet sinking.

Lucy stood still, up to her waist in water, willing me—longing for me—to learn, it seemed.

She said, "Breathe in slowly."

I rose up. She looked away. "Don't let go of me," I said.

"I wouldn't let go for anything," she said. "Close your eyes."

"I can't quite."

As long as I didn't breathe too much, I could just lie there. It was an amazing feeling, nothing like being in a bathtub. My arms felt like jelly. I looked up at the fancy clock tower on Merrimack Mills—some declaration of Prosperity and Progress from a better time.

Lucy said, "Imagine that my hands, instead of holding you up, are really the only things holding you down. They are like anchors, heavier than water, keeping you attached."

After a bit, I started feeling weightless and peaceful in the stillness. The hot sky wrapped all around me except where the brick wall of the Merrimack soared straight up. I'd heard Noe Hathaway had been inside there recently. Word had it that those huge rooms that once held weave machines as big as my room were vacant except for leaves that had blown in some broken windows. The whole concern had moved south. He said the place was quiet except for those leaves scraping the floor.

I closed my eyes. The water washed all the heat and sweat away. I imagined little waves slapping against my sides. I was a shell as empty as the Merrimack, all filled with air. Breezes blowing through—leaves sliding across the floor of me. I breathed and floated up. I let the air out, and sank a little, but not too much. Lucy's hands moved with me.

Far away, I heard one of the others, maybe Teresa, say, "She told me herself. It happened in Tallapoosa, Georgia." Lucy's grip tightened, and I popped my eyes open. It was like waking very suddenly from a deep sleep. She tipped me up, and I had to put my feet down fast. I stood, surprised, gingham plastered to me. She stared at the water, her eyes as big as a jacked deer's. I looked where she was looking: nothing but brownish river water and stones.

Teresa said, "Then they drove Edna out to who knows where, and the old man driving said, 'This is as good a place as any.' So they stopped and took Edna down from the back of the truck and threw all her stuff, even her radio and her shoes, down after her. They said, 'Don't come back, Edna Martin. Make no mistake: we don't want your union, and we are the Law here.' Then they drove away and left her somewhere near the border of Georgia and Alabama, all because she let slip to the boardinghouse owner in Tallapoosa that she was a CIO rep."

Katie asked, "Did they untie her before they left her?"

"I don't know." Teresa swatted at a fly pestering her mother. "She got back North all right, though. She's working over in Remington right now.

She says the Tallapoosa mill owner has everyone in his pocket: police, politicians, everyone; even the boardinghouse ladies."

Lucy hadn't moved. I asked, "You all right?"

They all turned to look at her. She turned red, and waded out. Her eyelids fluttered. She said, "I grew up in Tallapoosa."

Danuta asked, her Polish accent so thick she seemed to swallow her words, "Your family mill folk?"

Lucy said, "American Thread."

Katie asked, "What's the story, they want a union?"

"They need one worse than anybody." Lucy rolled her trouser legs down as if they weren't soaked through, hiding her face behind her hair. "But they're scared. People have been hurt."

We started back. Floorgirl was a job for people with no experience and no connections. Why would Lucy leave home when her family could get her a job, easy? My dress hugged me like a second skin and slapped my legs when I walked. I let the others get ahead of us.

"If your family's mill folks down where all the mills are moving to, what are you doing here?"

Lucy held herself as if her joints had seized up on her, and she didn't speak. She took that posture whenever O'Connor yelled at someone. I pictured Edna Martin, kidnapped and left on a country road all because a few boosters had gotten wind of her unionism. I asked, "Are you CIO?"

Lucy couldn't wear a poker face for anything. Right away, I regretted asking. I didn't want to get mixed up in any of that mess. Her feelings, or else her fight to beat her feelings, was all over her face. She wanted to lie to me. That was plain as day. But she couldn't.

"That's why you're all the time so damn dodgy."

She grabbed my arms. "Swear." Her nose flared, and her eyes filled. "Swear that's only between you and me."

I still have a snapshot of Lucy down by the river. She is waist-deep in that dirty water. Her hair hangs to her shoulders. She is holding me in the water, but you'd have to know that's what she's doing in order to find me in the swish of fabric floating in front of her. She has raised her face as if she's listening to something far outside the picture's frame. From this distance, anyone can see how lonely her secrets kept her.

⤳

Sometimes in the Knitting room, if we pushed all the big windows open as far as they'd go, a strong breeze would come through even in late summer. We'd imagine it brought whiffs of salt air. We'd think of a cool sandy beach where the Merrimack River finally flowed out to sea, where there was enough wind so seagulls could take it easy and just hang in the sky. But the week leading up to Labor Day, the air didn't move. Even with the windows wide, I felt as if my head had been stuffed with rags.

O'Connor asked me if I would train Lucy how to use a knitting machine. It meant I wouldn't make as much that week, but he knew I wouldn't squawk.

I thought she would catch on easily to knitting, but her machine kept getting all jammed up. She had to be doing something wrong. She kept showing me how she had done what she'd just done, and it looked right, but somehow the needles kept getting out of whack with the sinker bar. Every morning we went through the same rigmarole, checking the needles and getting any backed-up lint out. The longer it took, the more time I lost. The heat settled on me and flattened my hair. Maria Sarzana, Leona Pastana, Katie O'Neill—we all wilted over our machines.

When I'd taken Lucy's place at her machine for the fifth time that morning, she said, "If *you* ask, maybe O'Connor will get Noe Hathaway to take a look at it. I swear it's nothing I'm doing wrong."

Noe Hathaway was about the only one she didn't have a nickname for. He was a little man just begging for one. He had no teeth, shaved his head, and was bowlegged as a gunslinger. I'd interrupted her talking to him more than once in the stairwell.

He came through the door saying, "It's hot as a dye house up here."

O'Connor poured sweat from wheeling himself the twenty yards from the fan in his office. He said, "Forget your dye house. It's hotter than a two-peckered billy goat in this place," and wiped his face on his sleeve.

In the pocket of quiet from our two stilled machines, Noe began to take the circular head apart. He'd lost four fingers when he was a weaver. He'd worked in just about every mill in Lowell, and he could fix anything with those greasy stumps.

Noe looked over the top of his glasses at Lucy.

Lucy said, "Thank you for your help, Mr. O'Connor."

O'Connor said, "If it's all the same to you, I'm going back where it's a little cooler." O'Connor wheeled around and rolled back to his office.

As soon as the door closed, Noe said softly, "I worked a dye house over to the Merrimack. Did I ever tell you that story, Stella?" He paused while he unscrewed the swing plate. "The steam was so thick in that house that at first I didn't know anything was wrong. I could barely see my own hands, so I didn't know my buddy wasn't where he was supposed to be."

I couldn't help watching his hands work. I thought maybe he was going to tell how he lost his fingers. He lifted the needles one by one, slowly, blowing carefully at each bit of lint.

Like she'd got a pucker in her stitches, Lucy's face got all pinched together. "Go ahead, Noe. We don't have much time."

Noe continued a little more softly, "I nearly tripped over him. He was flat on his back on the floor. So of course, I tried to help him. But the floor boss . . ."—he shot a look at O'Connor's door—". . . he shouted, 'Get back to work, or you can walk.'" He widened his eyes at me. "My buddy died of a heart attack right at my feet because there was no union."

Noe finished, "I left that job the next day and went and found me a union." He held the circular head up between us and whispered, "See anything fishy?" He pointed with one of his stumps to two scrapes in the metal. "It's had pliers taken to it. Someone *wants* your machine to cast off unevenly." Then quite loudly he pronounced, "Lucy, I don't know why you think there's anything wrong here. I've taken the whole thing apart, and the only thing I can think is that you need more practice." He loosened the screw that had been tightened.

Lucy didn't let on. She grinned at me like a clown, as if she hadn't just learned that someone else must have known who she really worked for.

There was going to be a Company party the night before Labor Day. I thought it was a big deal. Lucy said it wasn't but a trinket tossed out by management to appease the workers.

I dragged her down to Merrimack Street past Sully's Tux Rentals and Arthur's Paradise Diner, where, these days, they sell a "Hub Mills Sandwich." The Bargain Box was a cute little used-clothing store with windows full of the latest in cast-off fashions. I opened the door for her. "We can snub our noses at the Junior League snoots who run the place."

"I thought we were going to the Dry Goods," she said.

"You got that kind of money?"

"I don't want to deal with the Junior League."

"I can handle them," I said, still holding the door.

She refused, like a dog pulling against its leash. I said, "Come on." I cocked my head at the dressy but headless mannequins in Sully's window. "You can't leave them lonely."

The Bargain Box was dark and crammed to the ceiling with clothes. The smell—something between mothballs and perfume—seemed like a promise. I led her to a rack of dresses.

Right off, a little blonde asked if we needed help finding anything.

I said, "No, thanks, doll," and sneaked a look at her hairdo. Definitely a salon job. I shifted through the dresses—some real possibilities—with Lucy hanging behind.

The blonde began refolding a perfectly folded pile of sweaters next to us. I thought with my tasteful hat I could have passed for someone who didn't need to shop there, but Lucy, Lord, with those brown slacks and her droopy hair, there was no mistaking her for anything but a mill worker. I said, "You'd think we'd be stuffing something under our blouses and making a run for it."

Lucy turned to the blonde and said, "What she means is that we are just looking, but will inform you as soon as we are in need of assistance. Thank you."

The girl nodded like a dismissed servant and went back to the cash register.

In a whisper, I asked, "How'd you do that?"

She didn't answer me.

"Where did you pick up that college voice anyway?" I pushed back the hangers to make viewing room.

She stared at the floor, holding her pocketbook like a shield, and turned ten shades of red. She whispered fiercely, "If you must know, my mother was in the Junior League."

You could have knocked me over with a feather.

"And just so you know, I don't want to wear a dress."

Junior League was for the wealthy women who wanted to look like do-gooders. But if you made anything of Lucy sharing tidbits of her past, she clammed right up. So I said, "What else are you going to wear to a party? You have to have a dress." I held one up to her—trying not to let her see how what she'd said about her mother had thrown me. "That one shows off your hazel eyes."

She avoided my face, and said, "Do you think?"

"Try it on." I held it out to her. "And try this bright green one, too, with the sequins." She took them from me without making a peep and headed for the changing room.

What if she lived in one of those houses with huge white pillars and big trees with creamy flowers like the ones in *Gone with the Wind*? The lawn would go on forever. There might be horses. A stable. Miles of white fence, and a big old turquoise swimming pool.

If that was how life was for her, then what was she doing telling Danuta her people were mill folk? I whisked through the hangers on the rack. I got to feeling itchy all over.

Maybe I was wrong to think we were friends. I told her everything, and what did she tell me?

She caught my hand as it madly flicked hangers. I hadn't heard her coming out of the dressing room. She slipped the sequined dress back onto the rack and whispered, "I've been afraid to tell anyone, even you. My father owns that mill, the one in Tallapoosa. American Thread. If anyone knew—you can see how that would go. There are just some things that shouldn't be said out loud."

She was still her soft-faced self, but everything about her had tipped off-kilter.

I turned her to face the mirror. I gathered her hair up off her neck into a twist and held it on her head as if she wore it in a chignon. Did I know her at all? With my free hand, I fussed with a hook that was loose at the waist. Lucy's eyes looked sadder even than usual. She checked herself up and down in that blue dress. Then she caught my eye in the mirror. Feelings crossed her face like clouds—like weather brewing—but I couldn't have said what they were.

To break the spell, I said, "I have some pop-it beads that would look nice. They'd show off your neck." I stopped myself saying, "Unless of course, you've got some pearls." I let go of her hair.

She said, "I'll take it. Let's get out of here."

While she was paying, I found a pair of shoes to match, but she refused to have anything to do with them because there was no Union Made sticker in them. Even secondhand, she wouldn't hear of it. "If I'd wanted to dance in nonunion shoes, I could have stayed in my daddy's house," she said. "I could still be living like a doll in a glass cabinet." She said all she had to do was think of Edna Martin, or any of the good people he'd put down, and know she'd rather go barefooted.

Lucy's room had the same inescapable view of the mill as mine. I'd decorated with postcards, pillow shams, and a bedspread to match—which was tits on a bull, if you think about it. Lucy's room was bare, except for books. She had more books than I had magazines. Her favorites were two dog-eared ones she kept by her bed: *Home Cooking with Mabel Lums*, and *Letters to a Young Poet* by some foreigner, and a slim little one she said was hot off the press, *The Golden Apples*, which she liked to read out loud.

I arranged just about every cosmetic I ever owned on her bureau top. "Come take a chair at Stella's Salon." I pulled her chair over. "That doesn't sound right. How about Stella's House of Beauty?"

Lucy said, "Stella's Shear Nonsense."

She wouldn't let me pluck her eyebrows. When I tried to curl her lashes, she acted like I meant to put her eyes out. She'd have nothing to do with bobby pins. "Why does everything have to be curly?" she asked. "I'm not a curly sort of person."

"Why can't you relax? Here," I said, pulling out her bureau drawer to make a footrest.

She pushed it back in and said, "I'm just as comfortable sitting up." I'd forgotten she kept that ledger in there. She squinted at me as if I'd gone out of focus.

Then she opened the drawer and pulled the ledger out. In the front, she was keeping track of on-the-job injuries, who got paid overtime, who didn't, who got paid vacation, and who didn't. The second part was a list. On each line was the name of someone employed by Hub Hosiery. She'd tallied who had joined and who would join a union. Lucy said, "The CIO is pushing to increase the number of organized plants." She said she was recruiting members, but there had been threats, so she'd been signing them up and collecting dues outside the mill walls.

She opened the bottom drawer and lifted a couple of folded towels to show off hundreds of leaflets. "Why Hub Needs a Union and How You Can Help." She said, "These are for when we move into high gear. I found a printer who did them up for free." She said that by sending a woman and trying a quiet approach, the CIO was still hoping to avoid violence. Management had people like Maria Sarzana on its side. Mr. Burroughs had seen to it that O'Connor gave Maria first shift so that she could be home with her kids after school hours, and in return, she was a company girl. "For her, an organized mill would mean she'd lose the benefits of being a favorite of the bosses." Lucy held the book out to me. "She may well be the person who messed up my machine."

There was my name in Lucy's script, *Stella Lewis* with no check in the yes or the no column.

"The more who say yes, the stronger we'll be. If you sign up we'll be one closer to moving in," she said.

"We have it pretty good, you know," I said. I didn't want to be on a list either way. Seeing my name there gave me the heebie jeebies. "We have jobs. Look what happened when the Merrimack organized."

"Management likes to keep that rumor circulating." She shut the book and slipped it back into the drawer. "The Merrimack Mill was moving down South either way. The bigwigs had already settled that."

I wasn't sure it made sense to go to work and then give money over in dues. What if some bigwig bought himself a car and had big times, spending and springing around with my money? I asked, "If I joined, who would know?" I pointed to the chair so we could get her made up.

"You and me, and one other CIO rep. We work in pairs." She sat. "In another month we'll be ready to make our next move." She picked up one of the lipsticks and read the bottom. "'Candy Apple.' Who names these things? I want that job." She twisted to look at me. "How long will I have to sit here?" She reminded me of my stepmother's goat, who used to push me off the stool just when I thought she was buckling down.

"You think this is going to improve me somehow?"

"Of course it is." I rubbed rouge into her cheeks. "You only want to put this up on your cheek bones so you emphasize the contouring of your face."

"You think I'm ever doing this to myself?"

While I did her lips with a creamy Revlon, she studied me. "So?" she said. "Are you in or out?"

"Does it matter to you, personally?"

"Very much."

I straightened up. "If it's that important, then I guess I'm in."

She looked at her hands in her lap and a lopsided lipsticked smile slid across her face.

I held the mirror up for her. She looked at herself carefully, turning her head, holding her chin up, and to the side. "Just like a monkey," she said.

They had the company bash at the Bonita Tavern. Who knows why a town on a river thinks it has to have a seafood joint, but it did, and the place was all gussied up in red, white, and blue, maybe left over from the Fourth of July. A little toy train, rigged out with dusty flags, *hoot-hooted* along the track that ran the length of the bar, dragging our drinks in a freight car. Cute. It was the sort of party where we drank a lot. Not that that excuses anything that happened. What a scene: cigarette smoke thick as fog, all of us girls dolled up, the men—at least some of them—in suits.

Lucy tottered to a table by the dance floor in my pumps, which were union made, but not to fit her. She put her elbows on the table and surprised me by launching into a speech. "Here, at the Hosiery division of Hub Textiles . . ." For an awful moment, I thought she was starting up about unions right there at the party. But she said, "At our annual fashion parade . . ."—she leaned toward a paper napkin dispenser like it was a radio microphone—". . . we are seeing a new and exciting trend in elegant wear."

She cut her eyes toward Johnny Frenier, who wore a suit that looked to be his father's. "The zoot suit has finally made it to Lowell." Lucy's deadpan got me laughing. She shifted her eyes right and left, mumbling like an undercover radio announcer into the paper napkins. "And look folks, here comes Bucky Thompson with, could it be? His sister?"

I had hoped he wouldn't show. There he came with, it must have been his wife. She looked just like him, tawny haired and jittery, with a cute little figure. I hadn't heard from him since the day I'd stood him up, and I had nothing good to say to him now.

To Lucy, I said, "You need a drink."

"I believe I'd like to try an Angel's Tit," she said, leaning back in her chair.

The smells of fried fish and cigarette smoke blanketed the crowded room. Billy Note and the Hi-Hat Band started up. Right off, Pete Jenks asked me to dance. I never learned anything but the polka and a Scotch jig when I was growing up, but I could fake a waltz. Pete stood a good couple of feet taller than me, but he smelled nice and only stepped on my toes once. After that, Stan Beecham wanted a dance. His hands sweated, and he kept wiping them on the front of his pants.

Lucy bowed in front of me and offered her arm. I laughed. Dolling her up really hadn't made her any more presentable. She looked like someone's maiden aunt. I should have insisted on the dress with the sequins. I'd made her up to be someone other than herself, and seeing how she didn't quite pull it off—how the dress she wore wasn't the best fit, and how my shoes did no favors for her legs—started something in me.

I sat down and watched people coming in. Just about everyone I knew crowded into that big room. I had never seen everyone in one place at one time before. O'Connor in his wheelchair patted as many women's bottoms as he could reach. Maria Sarzana limped on her lame foot. Katie O'Neill tried hard to look good in green. I was seeing, maybe for the first time, really seeing, the lineup of people I worked with. From their getups, you'd think the Depression had never ended in Lowell. The men joshed with each other and danced awkwardly with their wives. None of them had a full set of teeth. I felt embarrassed for them. But as I sat there, it came clear to me that this sorry-looking bunch was my crowd. I felt embarrassed for us all.

I'd thought I was different. No. Worse: I'd been convinced that I was better. The man for me was supposed to step through these people to find me. He would look something like Rock Hudson. Like me, he'd only be passing through Hub on his way to better things. Like me, he would be meant for a finer life, and he would want nothing more than for me to share it with him. I watched Pete Jenks dancing with Katie O'Neill and saw that she had had her wish come true. But all she'd asked for was a man tall enough so she had to reach to get her arms around his neck.

A fellow who looked like he'd just walked off the boat asked Lucy to dance. She craned her neck, looking for someone, anyone but him. Before too long, Noe Hathaway cut in. His head shone as if he'd oiled it. He looked natty for an old codger, like a cricket in a vest. Lucy danced as well as she swam, as if she'd had lessons—which she probably had.

I went to the bar, hoping someone would buy me another drink. The little train with its old flags tooted. I listened to two stocky fellows from the dye works arguing about the Red Sox and the Yankees. Katie and Pete danced past, then Sophie Robicheau and her bent old husband. I had on my best hat, but I was no different than any of them.

The fellow who'd danced with Lucy sat down beside me and leaned on his elbows. He looked Greek. His suit was so new that the thread from the tag still clung to the sleeve. His big tired features reminded me of the lion statues at Hub's front gate. He rolled his drink on his tongue as if he'd never had a Tom Collins before, and stared at the silly train chugging around the bar. His hands were huge and scarred. Everything about him, but his clothes, looked beat up or worn out. I turned away. It wasn't my night.

Lucy stood with Noe in a dark corner, their backs to the dance floor. Lucy's hands flew around while she talked. She was even further off course than I was. She'd left a life with swimming and dance lessons, of being taken care of. She'd *chosen* to be at Hub.

The man beside me stood and bowed slightly in my direction. Looking over his shoulder at the ceiling like he'd find the right words there, he pronounced, "Would you?" He placed his big hand on my arm. His accent made each word as carefully put together as a whole idea, "Please dance."

I'm not sure why I said yes, maybe because he and his cheap new clothes hit me as just the perfect punishment for someone like me, who thought she was better than everyone else. I said yes because I had no one but myself to blame. He smelled of gin and bacon.

The band played a waltz. He was broad-chested and solid. Anyone could see that his new shoes hurt. We spun until Lucy, watching from the edge of the floor, became a blue smudge.

After that, they played a jazzy two-step. I faked it. He did, too, and smiled at our trickiness. Before the dance was over, Lucy stood in our path. To my surprise, she introduced us. "Stella, George Kritikos."

He bowed low to Lucy, with Old Country grace. He stayed down there until she tapped him on the shoulder. "You don't have to do this every time you clap eyes on me."

He trapped her hand in both of his and said to me, "She saved my baby, Constantine." His eyes crinkled at the corners. Why did men get all the good eyelashes?

Lucy said, "Please excuse us, George," and hooking arms with me, marched me off the dance floor.

"What are you doing?"

"The question is, what are *you* doing?" She propelled me into the ladies' room and faced me. "Don't you know who he is?"

"No." I turned to check my hair in the mirror. "Who put the burr under your saddle?"

She grabbed my arm and spun me toward her. "That man is the baby's father and no one you want to have anything to do with." Her face swamped red.

I took my arm back. "Calm down."

"That man has a wife and a baby at home. A pregnant wife and a baby not even out of diapers."

"How choice—a family man." I refreshed my lipstick. "Even more perfect than I knew."

She was all business then, her eyes flat and dark and huge, like when she had jumped into the canal. "That isn't the half of it." Her hair was slipping out of its bun. She didn't know how to stand in heels—she was the picture of a dish ready to fall right off its shelf and smash on the floor.

"I'm only dancing with him," I said.

"You're not anymore."

"A bad two-step with me isn't going to break up his home."

"That's not it," she said.

"Don't bother. His company suits me tonight. That's all." I opened the door. "And don't tell me you have any better reasons for the choices you've made." I turned from her, probably too quickly, but it was done, and the ladies' room door shut between us before I could think about what I'd said or the frostiness I'd said it with.

George Kritikos was waiting for me. He could well have stolen his clothes. I sat with him at the bar. Stan Beecham bought me a drink, but I didn't feel like dancing. Kritikos was happy to sit silently. He closed his eyes. The place seemed tighter, as if the ceiling had lowered, closing us in with the smells of smoke, fish, and perfume. I had nothing to say to anybody and nothing to lose. Maybe Kritikos was drunk. What did I know?

He opened his tired eyes, ran his outsized hands through his hair, and asked, "You are always American?"

"Far as I know," I said.

He said, "This means you have good job. I see this." He nodded. "Greeks have not so good. But then things happen to get better."

I said, "You're a philosopher."

He wanted to know where I'd come from and who my friends were. He asked what was my opinion about this Union that people were talking about. "Is Lucy Mattsen good friends to you?"

"She's my best." I sipped my drink. "Or was."

Lucy sat at the corner of the bar. I could feel her eyes boring into the side of my head, but I wasn't going to look at her.

George Kritikos said. "Please to dance." He took my hand. I shook my head.

He said, "I persist." Of course he meant insist, but persist was true. He was using himself up by living his life—you could hear it in his struggle for every word, see it in the scars on his hands, the bags under his eyes—but still, he was curious about me, and even with sore feet, he wanted to dance with me.

I polkaed with him. He got my waist in his big hands, and took off. Dizzy, I began to feel lighter. It was good to be held that way. The smoky room whirled away and seemed larger, airier. The people blurred into splotches of color. I couldn't judge them then. Dancing, I got to feeling light as a wishbone, as if nothing really mattered.

I don't know when Lucy left. When the band stopped playing, I walked with him down Market Street, our shoes *tock-tocking* over the bridges in the quiet of the late night. You can hear the water flowing under the city that time of night. Two rivers and all those canals, gallons and gallons of water moving through.

The air had cooled. He gave me his jacket. I picked at the thread that hung from the sleeve. Walking with him felt more like the end of something than the beginning of anything else.

We turned toward the Merrimack on Cabot Street, where, from a radio in a darkened window Nellie Lutcher sang, "Come on-a My House." The Strand Theater was shut for the night. Kritikos said, "You aren't like the others," and stopped walking. "I see this immediately." He rolled his eyes to the streetlight as if he pulled his words from there. His black hair shimmered like a pelt. He took my wrist and guided me under the theater marquee, which boasted, "The Wonder of Stereophonic Sound Gives Realism to the Miracles of Cinemascope." Behind him, Loretta Young, in a maid's uniform, advertised *The Farmer's Daughter:* the movie Bucky and I didn't see. George pulled a pack of cigarettes out of his pocket and squeezed my elbow. He leaned to look at my face. "You have light."

I started to look for my matches.

"No." He showed me his own. "Inside you is light, shining. I see into you."

"What is it, exactly, that you see?"

"That you are lucky in love."

"No one has ever said *that* before."

He said, "You are here, no?" He stepped closer and drew on his cigarette, looking down at me as if he owned what he saw.

George Kritikos wasn't what I'd planned. I'd believed I was too good for his sort. Now, I wanted to see myself the way he did. Maybe it sounds like I am looking for excuses. I kissed him because he wanted me to, and there was no way for me to confuse what was happening with my silly ideas of how life was supposed to be. He wanted me, and he was as far from my cockeyed dreams as I could get.

~

The next morning, Lucy, in her usual brown slacks and sweater, slept against my door, her legs pulled up to her chest, her lips pouting comfortably against each other.

The hallway smelled like mildew. I put my hands to my cheeks to cool them, and hoped hard that the sleepy gray light from the stairwell window was dim enough that she wouldn't notice the state I was in. You could hear the hum of the city waking up. A dog barked once. Church bells rang for the early Mass. Lucy's head drooped heavy as a seedpod on a stalk. If she hadn't been in my way, I would have left her alone.

I squeezed her shoulder.

Her eyes worked hard under her lids, then blinked open. "I was waiting up for you."

She stretched her neck one way, then the other, and yawned. Her mascara had smudged to raccoon eyes. She pulled her watch out of her chest pocket, looked blankly at it, and stuck it back in again. She said, "You wouldn't listen."

"I heard you last night."

"No." She took my hand, and I pulled her up. She stood stiffly. "No, Stella." She had my hand by two fingers and tugged it up and down in an odd, hopeless way that bothered me. "What did you tell Kritikos?"

I fished in my handbag for my key. "I told him you'd taught me how to float."

"Good." She rubbed her eyes. "But remember how I wanted to go see the baby after he fell?" She was blocking my door. "There was more to it. The next day, I got Kritikos's name and found their apartment."

I kept my head down and went to the side of her to put the key in the door.

She said, "I thought Kritikos and his wife were likely to help us organize. If Kritikos was so tired that he could sleep through their baby falling out a window, management was taking advantage." She trailed in behind me. The place was stuffy with the smell of lavender soap. My hats were all over the bed—leftovers of my hopes for the party. I kept my back to her and heaved open the window to the morning, as if that would bring a fresh start.

"The baby, Constantine, was fine, like a little prince, pulling himself up and standing. But Kritikos didn't want to hear what I had to say. He kept saying, 'Mr. Burroughs will see to everything. Everything is good now.'"

With Lucy nattering on, I couldn't quite hold on to what I'd done. George Kritikos had made love to me frankly, as if that was what we both expected.

"Burroughs had gotten there ahead of me." She slipped a folded clipping from her pocket and held it out to me.

It was a photo from the *Lowell Sun* of George with Mr. Burroughs and the baby. Burroughs had his arm around George like an old war buddy. The caption said, "*Mr. William Burroughs, Jr., of Hub Textiles, with George*

Kritikos, whose baby was rescued from the canal yesterday by one of Burroughs's Hosiery division workers."

"That poor baby has to go through life with the name Constantine Kritikos. Can you imagine?" I said, handing the clipping back to her, and taking my shoes off.

Lucy closed her eyes and pinched the bridge of her nose. "Kritikos isn't working night shift anymore," she said. "Burroughs gave him second shift, so there's no more sleeping while his baby does things he shouldn't."

"Another happy ending."

"Don't you see?" She took a weary step closer to me. "Kritikos made a deal with the devil. He's a company man."

"Don't be silly."

She looked at the floor, and I thought she would never say another word. Then she came toward me. "Ask him where he got the money for his party clothes."

I pushed the hats out of the way and flopped on my bed. "How do you know Burroughs didn't just buy something nice for a fellow who almost lost his son?"

She crossed the worn boards in front of the window. The sun had made it over the mill walls and lit her up from behind. I had to squint through my headache to see her. "Mill owners," she stopped. "Don't ever do anything just to be nice, Stella." She jabbed her finger at the clipping. "See who is and who ISN'T in this photograph? The *Sun* might as well have said it was Mr. Burroughs who jumped into that canal. Why do you think Kritikos went for you last night?"

"Why wouldn't he?"

"Why do you think he was there without his wife?"

"Someone had to watch the baby?"

"And why do you think Kritikos asked so many questions?"

"Lucy, that's what you do at parties."

"He'll use you, if you let him." She seemed more sad than angry. "George Kritikos is a stool pigeon."

The last few hours came alive and crawled around inside me, but I said, "I don't buy it. I don't plan to be seeing him again, anyway."

"It's what he plans that matters. What would *you* do for double pay for overtime? Soon, he'll be sniffing around, asking when are Lucy and Noe Hathaway going to make their next move? What are they planning? How many can they count on?" She knelt by the bed. She was so close I could feel the breath of her words. "One slipup and they'll fire me, Stella. They'll stop us in our tracks." She bit her lower lip and cupped my cheek with her hand.

Trying to focus on the wash of freckles across her nose, I looked back at her like I hadn't been out all night and my face wasn't red with beard burn.

"You went to bed with him." She stood up. Her shoulders sagged worse than my mattress. The sadness in her turned-down eyes wasn't coming just from their shape. "How could you?" She passed her hand over her face, a strange, slow gesture. She crumpled the clipping. She jammed it into my wastebasket on her way out. She didn't even shut the door.

George Kritikos gave me no reason to ask why he did what he did. No red-blooded man would have done any differently, given the chance.

All the next week, Lucy avoided me. She kept her eyes on her knitting machine and her thoughts to herself. Her hair hung down over her face. O'Connor yelled at her more than once, calling her Grandma Molasses.

Once, I caught her with Noe in the stairwell. She paced on the landing and said, "Damn it all to hell." Then she saw me, shut up, looked at the floor, and waited for me to pass.

Rumors whispered their way through the mill. People were saying Maria Sarzana was going to get two weeks paid vacation, O'Connor's medical bills were being taken care of by Mr. Burroughs, Charlotte Stackley's daughter, who had no seniority, had been hired to be Mr. Burroughs's secretary, all sorts of rubbish like that. The whispering didn't get to me any more than Lucy's snubs did. I couldn't pay attention to anything but the slow syrupy feeling of Kritikos sliding his lips from my thigh to my belly. The memory went through me like a shiver through the side of a horse.

He'd undone me. I couldn't remember a time when I'd thought, yes, this is what I want—but I'd think of the way his eyes looked for mine and what it felt like to be *seen* that way, and I'd be off again, piecing that night into a good thing, bit by bit.

The hot day that Noe set up a jerry-rigged information table in the mill yard, people weren't working any harder than they had to, and no one said much. The effects of the party hadn't lasted long. Resentment ran through the mill sure as a vein of marble through granite.

On my way back from the ladies' I slowed by the bank of windows—hoping in vain for a gust of air. The sky, low and hazy, held out for a shower. From below, I heard cracking wood and a crash.

Down in the yard, Ted Thibodeau, the maintenance man I'd admired the day Lucy saved the baby, had pushed Noe back into the table—which collapsed under him. About a million pieces of paper slid every which way under Noe's efforts to get up. Lucy's fliers.

Thibodeau wasn't any bigger than Noe himself, but he had the advantage of being young and spry. He jumped on Noe and commenced to hitting him with a stick—a broom handle, it looked like. Noe tried to fend him off, but he had nothing but his hands with those stumpy fingers to fight with. Thibodeau hit him wherever he moved.

I didn't decide to step away from the window. It just happened, like when you step back from a too-hot fire. Lucy saw me, and she ran for the window. I tried to stop her, but she dodged me. I grabbed her around the middle. Even now, I am not sure why. She dragged us to where we could see Thibodeau going at Noe the way you'd beat a rug.

People crowded in one end of the patchy yard inside the brick wall, but for some reason, no one moved to help. Lucy broke free of me and made for the door, but O'Connor had wheeled himself square in her path. She could have darted around the bays and come at the door that way, but she flew at O'Connor, grabbed the handles of his chair, and flung him out of her way. He had no choice but to career into Luellen Michael's machine and crash over onto the floor. Maria Sarzana pulled on O'Connor like a sack of rice, trying to get him up, yelling for someone to put his chair right.

In the mill yard, something held everyone back. Ted Thibodeau had broken the broom handle against Noe by then, but kept on hitting him with the butt of it. The folks who'd gathered in the yard shot frightened looks at something directly below the window.

It was Kritikos—I knew that pelt of hair—and he wielded a metal stool like a lion tamer, swinging it and jabbing the legs at anyone who made a move to help Noe. My insides lurched, and I don't know what kept me from vomiting.

Lucy flew out the downstairs door. When she saw Kritikos, she slowed, circling but keeping her eyes locked on his. She was half his size. They could have been doing a circle dance, she in those sorry-looking shoes of hers—except her face pulled tight, and the only music was the steady drumming of Thibodeau's broom handle on Noe Hathaway. As

Kritikos followed her with the stool legs, I said out loud, like a lopsided prayer, "She saved your baby."

When Lucy spun away from him and jumped on Thibodeau, Kritikos didn't stop her. Noe'd quit fighting back. Lucy tried to grab the flailing broom handle or Thibodeau's arm, anything. He went at it like he was the one who kept the world spinning. He turned, trying to get at whoever was slowing his progress, but when he saw it was a woman, he stopped. He looked down at Noe—who was all over blood like something in a slaughterhouse—and he took off running. Kritikos headed in the side door to the office, still carrying the stool, leaving Lucy with Noe—what was left of him. She talked to him and made as if straightening his shirt would fix his face.

I slid down the wall by the window. Maria Sarzana wheeled O'Connor into the freight elevator. He held a blood-soaked handkerchief to his forehead. Everyone else had cleared out down the stairs. I stared at the big room of machines, the pillars and pipes, our empty apron pegs along the far wall, the greasy paper lunch sacks and thermoses by our chairs, and the pinup girl in pink garters on O'Connor's door. The blades of the ceiling fan twirled and twirled, easy as a lazy Susan, serving up whatever would come next.

⌒

The mill owner, Mr. Burroughs, in his three-piece suit, stood by the windows to talk to us. He spoke quietly—someone used to being in charge. I didn't see Lucy anywhere. Mr. Burroughs had brought his son, Dr. Charlie Burroughs, a fine-looking man, who wore tweeds and a bow tie. Katie O'Neill whispered to Teresa Bukowski that she'd heard the young doctor was still in training. He didn't know where to look. Those handsome eyes followed the pipes from the ceiling to the wall and couldn't settle any one place. He told us that Noe Hathaway wasn't conscious and so wasn't feeling any pain. Dr. Charlie Burroughs said that no one could say whether Noe would pull through or not.

When his son's gaze fastened on the floor, Mr. Burroughs stepped forward and said that the Burroughs family would make sure Noe had the best care possible. He said we should be proud that our socks carried the Hub seal on each and every arch. Our work was important during the war, and our veterans needed to know they could still get the same quality product they'd come to rely on. He talked about the years of dedicated service Noe had given to the company and asked if there was anyone whose machine hadn't been tended by him. Which of course there wasn't. Mr. Burroughs said that his prayers were going out to Noe with ours.

If Lucy'd been there, she might have said—out the side of her mouth— Doesn't the whole concoction remind you, just a little, of the recipe for an Angel's Tit? But she wasn't there, and I didn't know where she'd gone.

Lucy didn't answer when I knocked on her door. It felt like the room had been sitting silent for months, nothing happening but dust falling. Standing in the hallway, smelling the pasty scent of the walls, and knocking and knocking, I knew she wasn't in there.

I went back to my room and fell into bed, still in my clothes. I dropped into an exhausted, dreamless sleep that didn't last. Sometime in the middle of the night when the only lights shining were the mill's, I woke knowing I had to see the inside of Lucy's room.

I crept down the hall. Her door swung open on a dark and empty space. I flipped on the wall light. The mattress was bare, the pillow tossed onto the foot of the bed. I was suddenly sure she'd been run out of town the way Edna Martin had been, with all her belongings thrown into the road after her. But that was just midnight thinking.

The window was closed and locked. She'd had time to be thorough. Maybe even while Mr. Burroughs and his son spoke, she'd gathered her things. Her brown sweater and a couple pairs of slacks. Her accounts ledger and hairbrush. Her books. I searched her bureau drawers, which smelled only of themselves—cheap pine. I checked under her saggy mattress. I don't know what I thought I'd find.

I could imagine her carrying her suitcase quickly down those creaky stairs in the smudgy light from the hall window. I came up short, though, when I tried to think what she was thinking as she propped that book she loved so, *The Golden Apples*, against the mirror. She was proud of that book because a Southern woman had written it. She was always wanting to read it to me as if she'd written it herself. I thought I'd find an address inside it, a message, some way of finding where she'd gone. I upended it and splayed the pages out, but there was nothing.

The only other trace of her was the blue dress. She'd left it hanging in the closet like an accusation.

I muddled through the next days and weeks. O'Connor had seen me trying to stop Lucy from getting to the mill yard, so they didn't fire me. I tried to keep my head down and my machine's needles clear of lint. People whispered when I walked by. I'd worked there before I'd known her; why couldn't I keep on?

Too much had got all mixed up together inside me. Had Noe just followed orders from the higher-ups in the CIO, or did he go off half-cocked because of me? Had he brought the campaign inside the mill walls in a hurry because he didn't think I had the sense to keep a secret? There was no one to ask. Could I be responsible for the way someone judged me? Was it my fault that Noe was attacked? I couldn't catch hold of the answers. What I thought I knew slipped in and out of my head fast enough to make me sick and dizzy.

Instead of sleeping at night, I tried to come up with what I'd say to Lucy. I'd surely hear from her. She couldn't have gone far, maybe over to Remington, or up to Wamsutta over the New Hampshire border. It was a matter of time. Then, as if Lucy had died, someone else moved into her room.

⌒

I keep the book she left behind in the magazine rack at the salon. I keep hoping, as I comb out a client's freshly washed hair, or roll and pin her curlers, that the next girl, waiting her turn, might get curious and discover the stories in it. I still think of the times Lucy came to my room to read to me from it. She lay on my bed with one arm behind her head. She read and read to me in her Georgia slow-talk. One time I was seeing if Maybelline mascara—that old waxy block in the red case—did what it promised. I balanced it on the edge of my sink and wet the little brush. She rolled over and propped herself up on her elbows so her back bent like a spoon.

> Easter's hand hung down, opened outward. Come here, night, Easter might say, tender to a giant, to such a dark thing. And the night, obedient and graceful, would kneel to her. Easter's calloused hand hung open there to the night that had got wholly into the tent.

I liked it, letting the words flow over me while I brushed my eyelashes.

Nina let her own arm stretch forward opposite Easter's. Her hand, too, opened, of itself. She lay there a long time, motionless, under the night's gaze, its black cheek, looking immovably at her hand, the only part of her now which was not asleep. Its gesture was like Easter's, but Easter's hand slept and her own hand knew—shrank and knew, yet offered still.

Her reading was like having a radio playing, but as if it played only for me.

In the cup of her hand, in her filling skin, in the fingers' bursting weight and stillness, Nina felt it: compassion and a kind of competing that were all one, a single ecstasy, a single longing.

When Lucy was done, I asked, "Do you like it parted this way?"—I showed her my hair—"Or like this?" I parted it in the middle, and stood for her.

Her eyes settled on me, stilled there, taking me in with a look I'd seen before and didn't know how to read. I just thought she was trying to educate me in the stuff she cared about.

One whole wall of the salon is mirrors, just the way I used to imagine it would be. I've seen a lot of people's faces reflected there. Some of my regulars are men—like Pete Jenks, whose thinning hair I've been trimming ever since he married Katie O'Neill. Some of the boys from the State College have come to me for all four years they're in Lowell. One of them came back last week so I could be the one to give his baby her first haircut. George Kritikos's boy, Constantine, once came for a buzz cut, and I told him the story of when he was a baby and fell out the window into the canal.

But most of my clients are women. They share their plans and heartaches with me. Countless times I've watched a woman settle into one of the salon chairs, clutching in her hand a dream picture from a magazine, in her heart high hopes that a new cut or color will make her into the woman she'd always hoped to be. I can sympathize.

Not too long ago, a woman walked in who had that sadness in her. She didn't look like Lucy, but she had the same fine dark hair.

I couldn't comb out her hair like it was any old hair. When I tried, my hands shook. I had to ask one of the other girls to take over for me. I took my shaky hands into the salon's back room and tried to pull myself together. I don't know what they must have thought.

I have to live with this: I won't ever be able to tell her that I'm sorry about what happened. I wish I could have seen her for who she was—her whole complicated, funny, private self—before she was gone.

Remembering her face now is more and more like imagining. I can get the spray of freckles, or her round cheeks, or the sad corner of her eye right in my mind, but they melt before I can put them all together over her little chin.

What has stayed with me, though, along with my regrets—what I hang on to still—is what it felt like to float for the very first time—to lie back in the dirty, cooling water of the Merrimack River and learn that with every breath, I could rise up.

Blue Tango

"DELIA?" DR. CHARLIE BURROUGHS RAN HIS HAND OVER THE BACK OF HIS head, feeling the close cut of his hair. He looked behind him down the hall to the kitchen. The daylilies on the hall table had had it. Their green sticks stuck out at angles, brown-tipped. The spent blossoms had plopped down in their orange dust.

He followed the smell of coffee into the music room. She wasn't there. A silver pillow had rolled onto the floor by the sofa. He thought he'd find her sitting with her back straight in her satin robe, drinking her coffee, black, thick, the way she liked it. Or standing by the French doors, squinting against the steam from her cup and the sun's glare. Her black hair would give off the fresh smell of shampoo.

He had to concentrate to see the room, not as he'd carried it in his mind, but as it was at that moment. He wanted to confirm it all, touch the binding of every one of the books on the shelves, smooth the summer slipcover over the sofa, feel the cool wide boards under his feet. She would say he was being sentimental, but he wanted to breathe the dusty old leather smell of the encyclopedias. He yearned to be rid of the hollow feeling he'd hauled with him for the thirteen months he'd been away.

Sometime before 'dawn, he'd stumbled onto the bed. It wasn't what he'd planned. He'd wired ahead for her to expect him on the evening train from New York, but she hadn't met him at the Lowell station. He'd taken the edge off his feelings waiting in the station's bar.

When he'd fallen onto the bed, her narrow body had tensed under the covers. She'd said his name like a question. Afraid he'd weep, he closed his eyes and breathed her salty smell. The whiskey he'd had swirled in his head. Not sure he wasn't dreaming, he'd put his nose in her neck and careened into sleep like a long-distance runner collapsing across the finish line.

Now, except for the abandoned coffee cup on the end table, there was no sign of her. He didn't remember her getting up. He scooped the pillow from the floor, surprised by the coolness of the nubby raw silk, and tucked it into the elbow of the loveseat. They'd been married a little over a year when he enlisted. She'd found his sense of duty "misplaced." She'd said, "Just because you weren't trained in time for the last war doesn't mean you have to sign up for this one. Who cares about Korea?" But for him, it was important, above all else, to do the right thing.

Hot yellow light streamed in through the French doors. Charlie swung them open. The cat-stench of boxwood bushes poured into the music room. From the minute he'd left home, he had missed these smells of boxwoods, and parsley—and pungent marigolds. Now they pulled him with a force like gravity into this room, this view, this air. Stationed just south of the 38th parallel while the fighting raged at Hill Eerie and the peace talks dragged on, he had held himself apart from the others in his medical unit because of the uncontrollable strength of his homesickness. There were whole days he'd been unable to speak for fear of breaking down. Now, he breathed the sun-washed air of Belvidere Hill deeply, gratefully, and wouldn't care if Delia called him ridiculous. His grandfather, founder of Hub Mills, had built this Georgian-style house on the avenue lined with other Lowell mill owners' homes. Charlie remembered riding his tricycle in the shade of the copper beeches his grandfather had planted out front. The place had been special to Charlie for as long as he could remember.

Out beyond the asparagus hassocks, Canaday, the gardener, straightened his back and stretched. The asparagus glittered with dew. Cat briars had taken over the back corner. Now that Charlie was home, there was nothing to stop him from reclaiming that garden space. He'd take a little time before he returned to his post as internist at Lowell City Hospital. Working alongside Canaday, he would sweat, clearing the tangle.

He looked for Delia in the kitchen. The room was different, harder, brighter than he remembered. She'd had a gleaming copper hood installed over the oven, and shiny new pots hung from an iron rack. There he was. The shape of his rumpled uniform, topped off by his pale face and dark hair, shone back distorted in miniature—in triplicate, quadruplicate—a battalion of wrung-out little Charlies shone from the pot rack. Maybe she'd gone out to give him time to pull himself together.

He stepped out into the drive and found the Bel Air in the garage. Wherever she'd gone, she must have walked. He imagined her taking long strides under the sprawling shade trees, past the trim hedges of sunny Fairmont Avenue on her way down the hill to the corner store—the lithe lines of her, the symmetry of her lean face, her pulse beating in the tender skin below her ear. She'd swing her bare arms, the hot sun on her face, her skirt swishing declaratively. She walked the way she thought, in a straight clear path. She sliced through life, clean-edged.

Charlie turned back to the house. He had made pictures like this for himself so many times while he was away, but now, here, home in Lowell, his imagining came so close. She'd wired him, finally: "How much longer will you be gone?" He carried the telegram in his breast pocket like a tattered ticket back to his life. She could appear any second.

⤳

Charlie and Canaday concentrated on the rhythm of their work. With Canaday, Charlie could pick up where he'd left off. Stripped to their undershirts, Charlie swung a scythe, and Canaday, built like a barrel, used a machete. They hacked away steadily at the back corner of the extensive garden until Canaday swore, "Damn briars." The words released Charlie to step up the pace. Working fast distracted him from watching for Delia.

When they had the stalks to stubble, bristly and trampled, they went at it with shovels, stamping the blades in, severing roots. Charlie got hold of one of the roots and yanked, plowing a diagonal line through the patch, toppling stalks.

Canaday said, "Knee bone connected to the thigh bone," and slapped his ham bone, smiling.

Sweat dripped down Charlie's temples. The repeated slide of metal into dirt, and the *thunk* of shovel cutting root resounding in his arms should have satisfied him. He wanted to feel satisfied in his body. It had been a long time since he had. Between breaths, he asked, "Did you see Mrs. Burroughs go out this morning?"

Canaday looked quickly to the corner heap where he'd stacked the cracked clay pots. Then at the hole worn in the thumb of his work glove. He was no good at hiding his feelings when someone's eyes were flat on him, and his intolerance for Delia was as sure as an old dog's for a new cat.

"On her bike. She's a regular trick rider, that one."

Delia had a way of getting a running start and jumping onto her bike without touching the pedals. "Did she say where?"

Canaday shook his head and shifted his weight from his bad hip. He wiped his brow and looked at the sky, trying to keep from saying anything more. "Your wife has an awful lot of weather in her."

Canaday had probably kept his trap shut all these months. Charlie said, "Why don't you take a break." He could imagine Delia swishing into the garden shed—which Charlie's father had built to Canaday's specifications when Charlie was a boy. Delia would shout Canaday's name to compensate for his deafness. He'd restrain himself from shouting back that he didn't need an ear trumpet. She'd stand straight on her stalk, a good head taller than he, and remind him of something he hadn't forgotten but was getting around to in his own time. Delia expected to be indulged. (She'd been the youngest, the only girl among the Barnetts of the nickel mining fortune.) Charlie had noticed that her roses were in exceptional shape, and the garden gate didn't have its usual squeak. Canaday went for water, stumping between the reaching stems of bean plants.

A little breeze brought the blunt smell of the Merrimack River, riffled through mounds of growing parsley, and stirred up the tomato vines.

Beside Charlie, the junipers tossed their empty branches. He drove his shovel into the ground, and turned the earth. Shoveled and turned, hoping the rhythm of the work could fill the hollows in him, and make him know he was home again. His anticipation of how it would be made it hard to see how it was, exactly.

Where was she? Why had she gone? He wanted to do what was right. Should he go looking for her and start over? The first thing was to get beyond his passing out on top of the bedcovers.

Charlie pulled his shirt on. But what was he going to do, go calling for her through the streets of their Belvidere Hill neighborhood as if she were a lost dog? When he'd enlisted, she sat at the bottom of the stairs, leaning her head against the balusters like a dejected child. She wouldn't look at him. No matter what he'd said, she wouldn't see the necessity of his going.

He couldn't see how he'd had any choice. He was healthy and had the best medical training there was; he was an American man who believed in democracy; he loved his country; his country had called him to do his part against communism.

He brushed vaguely at the dirt on his knees. He'd wanted to feel really needed somewhere in his life. But what if he'd been wrong to think his country needed him more than she did? He ran his hand over the back of his head. From her letters, he would say that she'd gotten beyond his leaving. Hadn't she said she'd gotten used to not having him to talk to? What if all along she'd needed him more than he knew? He spun slowly in his garden, looking to the reach of sky, to the purple shadows in the juniper boughs, to the beech branches cascading above the walkway.

He looked around for Canaday, who was, for some reason, coming out of the house. With shame, Charlie knew he must look like a scarecrow twisting on a stake, waiting for the crows to come land on his hat.

⌒

Delia said, "No point in standing on ceremony." Barefoot, she pulled left-over lamb and mint sauce from the icebox. She wore a dress that accentuated her waist and hips, like those Charlie had seen on the women of New York City when he passed through.

Her appearance gave no clue to how she'd spent the day. Before she finally came around the corner of the garage, he and Canaday had worked the dahlia bed to where you'd want to reach in and let the soil run through your fingers. Charlie's relief at the sight of her sang through him. She'd seemed preoccupied—hadn't seen him off there in the back. She'd reached up and let the hanging beech whips slide slowly through her hand as she passed. He wouldn't ask where she'd been. She resented the way he arrived last night. And maybe he'd been wrong; she needed him more than he'd understood.

She passed him a plate and sat. She said, "I was taken aback by your telegram. I thought they'd keep you in California for formalities—whatever an honorable discharge involves." She peppered her meat liberally, and looked at her plate.

He must have searched the strangeness of a million faces in Korea looking for something of this one, this unique assemblage of eyes, nose, cheeks, and mouth. Delia. She had cut her hair so it framed her face. He looked at her teeth, remembering their little crookednesses, how his tongue knew their edges.

She looked quickly at him, and away. "I wasn't sure I was ready to see you." She sat on her hands, her arms close to her sides.

He got up to pour himself a scotch and soda. "I'm sorry. Last night was inexcusable."

She left her knife and fork where they were and lifted a slice of meat to her mouth with her fingers. She always said it tasted better that way. Flying in the face of customary behavior pleased her.

He took a sip of his drink, looking at her over the rim of his glass before sitting down. He wanted to kiss those fingers, to pull her to him, as he had dreamed and dreamed of doing. "That dress becomes you."

"Do you like it? I don't much. It's Christian Dior. I think it might look better in the window at the Bargain Box." She leaned for her dropped napkin. "It isn't me, really."

"They're wearing it in New York." When he'd thought she would come to New York to meet his plane, he'd pictured her in a dress like this, something fashionable, standing out tall among the other wives.

She let her head go to the side on her long neck, like a Modigliani. When she hadn't been at La Guardia, he'd imagined their reunion in the slanted light of the train station, how she'd tip her head just like that and smile. And that would be enough.

Remembering the silky feel of her skin, his body turned watery. He reached for her hand, but she was dipping a piece of meat in mint sauce. Her blush reminded him of her sweet stillness the last time he made love to her before he went away. Her face had turned slightly from him. He'd memorized that, how she held her passion just below the surface, like muscle under skin. Waiting in Seoul, he had gotten so sad and hungry with wanting her that he had gone to whores. It shamed him now to think of it.

"Delia. I have so much to ask your forgiveness for."

"You mean like that with the doors today?"

"Doors?"

"Weren't you trying to lock me out?"

"Why would I do that?"

She searched his face. "The music room door was the only one I could open."

"Why on earth would I do that?" He had the sensation of swimming in a new element—not quite liquid, but thicker than air.

She shifted in her seat. "I thought it was some sort of signal." Her skirt fabric shimmered under the kitchen light.

With some effort, he settled his fingers around the silverware her mother had left her. "I didn't lock the doors." It was possible Canaday had. Charlie set about cutting his meat. "Is there butter?"

She passed him a flat yellow cake of oleo. She tucked her hair behind her ear, and passed him the bread. Her slim hands moved with an efficiency he didn't remember. She pushed her thumb in little circles against the back of her other hand, rubbing in a smudge of mint sauce. Her eyes fixed on the wall behind his head.

She'd framed a print, a detail from the Tapisserie de Bayeux—a magnificent needlepoint panorama of the Norman Conquest, of hundreds of horses, their forefeet uplifted, bearing proud conquerors in their armor. The yarns they'd used were beautiful earth tones, the tawny color of her eyes, the dusk of her hair.

He turned and caught her composing the reflection of her face in the toaster. What had he seen there before she smoothed her forehead and set her lips? He didn't know. During the war, he had written her every day he could. He had kept to the benign, protecting her from the horrors by picking the harmless or amusing detail to share with her. He'd never been close enough to see the fighting, but he had lived with the bodies of those who had. He hadn't let her know of the exhaustion, his hatred of the Chinese reawakened every time he heard the helicopters, the bitterness he felt patching up men like so many blown tires, one after another, after another, day in and day out. Now, being near her, he was overwhelmed by how alive she was. He leaned across the table and took her face in his hands. He hadn't meant to be so abrupt.

She didn't meet his eyes, but wiped her hands on her napkin.

He let go. But her skin. He wanted to touch her all over. He loved the way her hair slipped out from behind her ear and she tucked it back.

She said, "It's . . . I'm not someone who should be left alone."

Charlie stood. What was happening was so far from what he'd been sure it would be like. He left the table, tipping into a welter of confusion. He was going about this all wrong. How ridiculous he must look, pouring more scotch when his glass was nearly full. He needed to slow down.

Turning toward the music room, he said, "Some music would be nice, don't you think?" Of course, she would need to be courted. Of course, she would need time.

In the music room, he sat hard on his piano stool. It was twisted up for someone shorter than he. Delia did not play piano. The shock of the truth traveled up his spine. Down his arms, to his hands, which stung. He gripped the cool, smooth seat of the stool. He stared, dizzily, at the scrolled *S* of Steinway, trying to steady down. The music on the stand was nothing he knew, some pop tune called "Blue Tango." It belonged to someone else.

She followed him in and lingered by the French doors, looking out at a robin on the lawn. It rushed and paused, rushed and paused. Her face was a practiced one, a beautiful closed face. She folded her arms across her breasts.

"How about Debussy?" he asked, his voice thick. He would not play Satie, his favorite. Not now. He adjusted the stool as if it were part of his everyday routine. She turned away from him, resting her shoulder against the glass of the door. The fabric of her dress rose and fell slightly as she breathed. She smoothed her hair, and her hand shook.

He started to play Saint-Saëns. He leaned into the music, trying to give his ear over to the swells and flow of it, trying to give himself over. Behind her, the garden hummocks were a soft blue-green. Dew would be gathering there. If he could make a space with the music, reshape the thudding of his blood. If this moment could only be the next one or the one after that, to take him beyond knowing that someone had been in his place.

She said, "Charlie." But he wouldn't stop. He couldn't. He closed his eyes. He felt her watching him for a long time, and then sometime, silently, on her clean, bare feet, she left the room.

After a while, he stopped playing. He sat until his drink was finished. The lilies Canaday had brought in were closing up. They smelled too sweet. He poured another drink. He tossed the telltale song sheet into the wastebasket and made his way upstairs.

Their bedroom, with its thick rug and plush dark drapes—all of the surfaces and edges softened—gave him no comfort. She wasn't there. Their bed, the old four-poster, hadn't been made. Her side was turned back where she'd slipped out that morning. He'd pressed wrinkles into the coverlet where he'd fallen.

What had she seen when she looked at him passed out there? Had she had to lift the drunken weight of his arm and leg off her to get up? Had it felt like lifting the limbs of a stranger? He imagined her slipping away from him—her skin sliding across the smooth sheet.

The night before, when the barman at the station, pouring him another double, had asked, "What's your destination, soldier?" he'd heard, "What's your destiny?" He hadn't known how to answer except with her name.

Her negligee had been flung onto the footboard. He lifted the hem and let it flutter back. The silky fabric slipped like water through his fingers. With a rush, he understood, again, something he had known once. Without Delia, he was without substance. Without her, nothing he did or had done mattered at all.

He straightened her hairbrush and comb on the dresser. He touched the soft dry back of her powder puff, and then closed the powder tin. Sandalwood. He looked out the window and down toward the river, where distant smokestacks from the mills poked the clouds. It was a quiet summer night on Belvidere Hill. An older couple walked under the street lamp below. The man wore a hat. The woman clasped her hands behind her bent back. Their retriever wove between the copper beeches.

He found his old tartan bathrobe hanging on the back of the bathroom door, as if he'd never been away. They had taken vows. Mistakes had been made, but they had taken vows. Now, he would do the right thing. Whatever it took. He was her husband, a man of his word.

First, he would take a bath. In unlimited hot water, as much hot water as he wanted to use. He twisted the faucet handle open and let it flow. He would find patience like that: he would be a man of unlimited patience. He pushed the black rubber stopper into place. The rush of water, the sound filling the room, comforted him. He would act with such forbearance; the clarity of his actions could not fail to define him. He held his fingers under the force of the water, and felt it warming, gradually, until it was good and hot.

After his bath, when he'd dried off, he would wrap himself in his tartan robe, open the windows, and climb into bed. His erection, he'd ignore. He'd prop himself on the pillows and breathe the night air of Fairmont Avenue. He would have a nightcap and listen to the crickets. Whatever it took. He would wait for her.

Glass Box

Delia Burroughs reached for the aunties' paprika, feeling she was on display, as if caught inside one of those mechanical scenes in a dusty glass box—each woman a gear that did its part, arms stirring, waists bending, opening the oven, closing the oven: "Working in the Kitchen" the typed label would read.

The kitchen had nothing in it that hadn't been there for centuries, except for an electric wall clock that hummed, and a radio that wasn't ever turned on. When Delia married Charlie, she'd had no inkling that this sort of day would have any place in her life.

Bess and Gwen Lathrop, Charlie's utterly threadbare relations, lived in a farmhouse surrounded by suburban development in the outskirts of Lowell not far from the Merrimack River. A few old apple trees and an outbuilding survived from the original farm. Their side of the family hadn't benefited from the mills as the Burroughs had. Fixing Sunday dinner, the sisters insisted on aprons over their church clothes. Gwen, always the frail and frilly one, had ruffles at her shoulders. The milky edges to her irises made it hard for Delia to look her in the eye. Bess had a curvature or something, so when she walked, her rib cage jerked out on the side opposite whichever leg stepped forward. They were both terribly skinny and quick and smelled of lavender powder.

"Delia, is Franklin doing something he shouldn't?" Bess asked.

In the pantry, Franklin, who was just a little more than a year old, squatted on his chubby legs, peering into a bag of potatoes as if it were a cave.

"He's fine."

Gwen pulled the cabinet drawers out of the built-in to make them like stair steps.

Delia said, "I can reach. What do you want?"

Gwen marched up the drawers. "No need, dear. It must be lovely to be tall, but we have our ways."

Whenever Charlie's chronic sense of duty brought him here, dragging Delia with him, he would set himself some impossible task to make a contribution to the meal. Today he was firing up the old wood-burning cook-stove in the outbuilding to make popovers, his latest specialty. Wearing his narrow-lapelled tweeds and a new tie from Brooks Brothers, he'd gone off with his supplies in a basket.

Delia imagined him in the dark old outbuilding, folding his jacket and rolling his starched shirtsleeves up. He always wore a jacket and tie; it was a given, as much as the old-fashioned code he lived by. He'd push the tail of his tie into his shirt to keep it out of the way while he checked his fire. The flames would light up his cleanly sculpted face, his square brow, and close-cropped hair. (He went to the barber every Saturday, and had a habit of running his hand over the back of his head.) He'd break the eggs for the popovers one-handed, *whap*, on the edge of the bowl. He wouldn't raise clouds when he whisked in the flour. She knew his routines. Charlie lived the script his parents handed him at birth. He was the second son in the third generation of mill owners and, according to family patterns, a doctor.

It was no surprise that he'd married her. From his first sight of her, which he counted as the most important turn in his life, he'd had eyes only for her. Eyes, and heart and mind, too. When she couldn't control her temper, he kept his head. When steadiness was what she needed, he lent his. Which made him mysterious to her. He was truly the best part of her. But today, he'd said, "I'd only be in the way if I tried to bake in the kitchen," and he'd left her with these women.

She heard the sack of potatoes rustling on the pantry floor. Franklin had found the only dirt in the house. She went to wipe his hands on her dress, but the aunts would want his hands washed. His head was really too big, she was afraid, even for a toddler. He had the same little extra curl to his left ear as she did, but she had to try hard to find something of Charlie's features in his. He swung his head from side to side, unbalancing her, and made his stocky little legs go like pistons so she had to put him down. He waddled right back to the potatoes.

Bess pushed in the drawers. Gwen cleared a place for the platter. The aunts could make her feel so unfit. In her own house, she was accomplished, slap-dash, unflappable, stylish. She was queen of her kitchen—could cook like no one's business. These people didn't know. At home she didn't wear clothes when she didn't feel like it, served dinner at midnight if that's what she wanted, and didn't care what anyone thought about her putting chocolates she'd bitten into back in the box. Maybe being the youngest and only girl had made her bratty and self-assured, but here, when she and Charlie pulled up, the aunts were out Hoovering the stone walk as far as the cord would reach.

Delia sat, looking out the window, hopelessly out of place. The arbor vitae hedge had been recently pruned to the quick. "Aunt Bess, did you ever call Wetherbee? Remember that yard man I told you about?" One way she'd learned to endear herself was to recommend people who could help. "He's awfully good at the heavy stuff."

Bess said, "Did we get in touch with Wetherbee? Lord, yes."

Gwen let go her hilarious laugh. It went up the scale like a bottle filling up. "He's in the living room."

"We couldn't do without him for a minute," Gwen said alarmingly, handing Bess the platter. "He's become like family."

Delia pressed her lips together.

Bess placed the deviled eggs in rows. Gwen placed the parsley garnishes. Their practiced hands wove in and out. Bess said, "He's such a find."

Delia had fired Wetherbee, her second gardener in as many years. And then, feeling guilty, had recommended him to the aunts. She pitched her voice low and sure. "What's he doing in the living room?"

"He usually reads the paper. He's come for dinner every Sunday since he started. Comes early." Gwen smiled, and her cheeks folded like sashed drapes. "Gives us someone to cook for."

Franklin pulled the potatoes one by one onto the floor. Delia said, "Franklin." Augustus Wetherbee was going to sit for Sunday dinner with them. "Come here to Mummy."

Franklin toddled toward her as fast as he could go, careening—she never could predict what he'd do—down the hall with the crooked pressed-tin ceiling and into the little living room.

Wetherbee lounged with the newspaper in the wing chair by the fireplace. Though he wasn't tall, his solid shape dwarfed the chair. His thick hand made the aunties' teacup look like a dolly's. (He drank coffee all day, Delia remembered, sometimes two mugs going at once, one in the garden shed, one balanced on the sundial in the dahlia bed.) As Franklin careened past him, his shorts sagging with the weight of his diaper, Wetherbee peered over the top of the newspaper: God the Father looking down through the clouds. He had old scars like a fighter and a nose that had been broken once. His eyes followed the little boy out into the hall. When he saw Delia, he stood. Wetherbee always wore work clothes, but for Sunday dinner with the Misses Lathrop, apparently, he wore clean ones. His blue eyes crinkled with . . . what?

"Mrs. Burroughs." He nodded.

"Wetherbee," she said, as if naming him would make him go away. She made herself look him in the eye. "Excuse me." Going after Franklin, feeling toppled, as if by a wave, she passed quickly through the other door.

She imagined him sitting back and breathing through his nostrils with satisfaction. He would have known, of course he would have known, that they were coming for dinner.

Charlie obliged the aunts by taking the seat at the head of the table. He helped pass the game hens and scalloped potatoes, the deviled eggs, and turnip. But because he hadn't timed them quite right—popovers had to be eaten piping hot or they got soggy—he'd jumped up from the table, and with his napkin still tucked over his tie, he'd dashed out again. Delia would just have to fend for herself. Wetherbee had placed himself directly opposite her in the narrow dining room. She had the sensation that the whole room tilted toward him, lace-covered table, homely highboy, candles. She felt the pull of him like an undertow and kept herself steady by looking at the lilac bush through the wavy glass of the old window—how its leaves, chalky with the lateness of the season, wobbled in the breeze.

Wetherbee told the aunts in his flat country accent, "I've always worked close to the land. I still remember the first time I helped with a calving on my uncle's farm in Tewksbury." He leaned back in the spindly chair. "The first thing he does, my uncle, is he gives me a glove that stretches clear up to my shoulder." He made a chopping gesture against his muscle where it strained the cotton of his shirt. The aunts stopped chewing. He turned to Delia. "If I remember right, Mrs. Burroughs, you have some slim black gloves that reach about yea high, but this glove wasn't as fetching as those."

The aunts seemed to have stopped breathing—perhaps rapt by the thought of Wetherbee reaching into a cow.

"Then my uncle hands me a chain, says he was only kidding about the glove; he'll take care of that part if I'll pull when he tells me."

Gwen laughed her bottle laugh with such relief that she sounded like she might just overflow.

Bess grimaced at Delia. "Isn't he awful?"

Delia took a black olive into her mouth and held it in her cheek. It gave her something to do with her face.

"So I took a-hold of that chain, and he wrapped the other end around the calf's feet." His meaty hands wrapped a chain around the air in front him like a conjurer. "You see, it was a breech birth; he was coming out ornery fashion, which Mrs. Burroughs knows all about. So I pulled with all my might." He patted his solid middle. "I wasn't full grown then. But that calf just popped out and slithered into a heap on the hay."

Gwen said, "So everything turned out all right," and smoothed her plaid skirt. They'd taken their aprons off at the last possible minute.

Bess said, "I didn't know Franklin was a breech baby."

"He wasn't." Delia handed Franklin a spoon, which he banged on the tray of the old high chair. "I'm not sure just what Mr. Wetherbee meant." She lifted her fork to her mouth. "This turnip is delicious."

Bess said, "Rutabaga, dear."

Charlie swooshed through the swinging door wearing oven mitts, bearing the cast iron pan of golden popovers. That morning she'd thought her husband looked handsome. He was built to make tweeds look fine. When he'd shaken hands with Wetherbee, Charlie's black eyes snapped, and she'd seen how strong her husband's features were, carved chin, forceful brow. Now he seemed slight, dandyish, and excessively proud of his popovers.

Bess oohed. Gwen hopped up for a knife.

Charlie said, "It must be very sharp, Aunt Gwen."

Such a production.

When Charlie freed the popovers from the pan, Delia cut and buttered Franklin's. He buried his face in it, getting his tongue into the buttery hollows. Wetherbee opened a popover, prying with his thumbs, gently separating the steaming skin at the center. He said, "Thank you, Dr. Burroughs." He buttered the halves, the silver butter knife ridiculous in his big, calloused hand.

Charlie said, "You're welcome."

An awkward silence followed. The aunties had set an atrocious table runner down the middle in an ochre-orange color Delia supposed they'd chosen to signify the fall season. The glaze on the old dinnerware had cracked into a pattern similar to the wrinkles on the old ladies' faces. Delia wondered if, at times like these, when fulfilling what Charlie deemed his familial duty, he wished he could be somewhere else, weeding his garden, or playing the piano.

Wetherbee asked, "Is there batter left? Mrs. Burroughs will say she's watching her wasp waist, but I could eat a couple more."

Charlie stood and gathered the pan and mitts. "Aunties?"

The aunts said, Oh no, they couldn't possibly.

Charlie looked at Franklin's greasy face and said, "If that child will leave us some butter, I'll bring a fresh round in a minute."

Delia wiped Franklin's face with her napkin. Butter clung even to his eyelashes. She glanced briefly at Wetherbee. Half of his popover sat untouched on his plate. Little spritzes and sizzles of the game he was pulling her into made her feel she could do with a nice cold martini. But the aunts were teetotalers. She tucked Franklin's bib in better and, once Charlie had left, said, "Did Mr. Wetherbee ever tell you about when he worked on the pig farm in Nova Scotia?"

Wetherbee's job had been to make sure the hogs mounted the sows successfully. He had once told her, "You know the tail? All the important parts of a pig, male or female,"—he'd drawn a curly-cue, slowly, slowly, with his finger on the inside of her arm—"are shaped like the tail." Delia remembered his thick finger tracing circles, how it had unmoored her. Standing in the garden shed in the backyard, she had tried to seem unaffected by the currents he'd set eddying in her. He'd said, "There's a reason they need full-time help." He didn't say that now.

"I worked up there the year you had that big storm here," he said, smooth as anything. "What was that one called?" he asked.

Gwen had her mouth full. Her eyes bugged with wanting to speak, to tell about the great storm.

Bess said, "Oh yes! That was before they started naming them. The hurricane of '38 was the worst. Father was still with us then." Her back straightened, excited. "A big old limb from the elm that used to grow out front came very near to flattening the porch." She glowed like a schoolteacher. "First there was an ungodly cracking sound as if the sky itself had split, then that great limb fell straight down." Her hand plummeted silently into her lap. "And missed the porch by mere inches."

Gwen nodded emphatically. "Mere inches."

Wetherbee appeared consumed with interest. His scars had fascinated Delia from the first, especially the way his nose angled down from the bridge, giving him a Mediterranean look. "And how did your neighbors fare?" He knew just what to ask.

Bess said, "No one had any serious trouble right around here, but the Oakleys' first cousins from Westerly all floated away in their house." She touched her napkin delicately to the corners of her mouth. "Sat down to Sunday dinner at their place on Napatree Point, just as we did here today, and that was the last anyone saw of them. Every last one washed out to sea."

Gwen said, "In the newspaper photo of the house drifting away, we thought—when we got out the magnifying glass—that we saw their pale faces peering from the attic window." She looked from Delia to Wetherbee. "Can you imagine?"

Delia said, as innocently as possible, "Was there some reason you had to be out of the country at that particular time, Mr. Wetherbee?" He'd once told her he'd been in a brawl, and a man had died. Wetherbee had been so drunk, he didn't know whether he was responsible.

Watching her over the rim of his water glass, he emptied it. Then he said, "Oh, it could have been any year." He didn't take his clear blue eyes off hers. "It was none too soon for me to get away."

Delia said, "But wasn't there some particular reason?"

"As these fine ladies know," he picked up his fork, "I was in need of reform. A hot-headed young man."

"It's hard to imagine," Delia said without inflection.

"He had to go away to learn temperance," Gwen informed Delia.

"So, you changed your ways?" Delia realized she had never seen Wetherbee drink anything but coffee or water. They'd always met during the day when Charlie was at the hospital—the aunts were right; there'd been no liquor.

"That was a long time ago," Wetherbee said casually. "Ancient history." He'd lifted her onto the guest bed, as if she weighed nothing. When he touched her, her body hummed, came singing up. He lifted her to the surface of herself—could make her feel inside out with wanting. Now, he pulled his chair closer to the table, closer to her, and asked, "Were you even in ankle socks then?"

She tried to sound breezy. "Now what would you know about the fashions of the times?"

Wetherbee said, "I rely on my ladies," he gestured toward the aunts, "for that." The aunts tittered. Bess adjusted her cardigan. Gwen smoothed her skirt. Delia used to feel so weak through the middle that her knees shook when he undid her buttons. She had to lie down wherever they were—in the shade of the hemlocks at the back of the garden, or in the music room where, as he opened first one side of her blouse and then the other, the full morning sun fell hot on her bare skin.

Charlie came in, bringing more popovers. Delia straightened up and said, "Why don't you tell us something about your growing up, Mr. Wetherbee. Were you very active in your church youth group?" She smiled at him. He turned his big head toward her, and it was as if her own center of gravity shifted. She knew, with her hand's own memory, the saltiness of his hair, the heat of his soft ears. She imagined how she would hold his head to her breasts. She would follow the curves of his thick shoulders and back with her hands, like water over falls.

"Isn't that about when you met Mr. Burroughs for the first time?" he asked.

"Oh tell," said Bess.

"Yes, do," said Wetherbee.

Franklin started to fuss and wriggle out of his chair. Delia stood to put his pacifier in his mouth. Her neck and then her cheeks flushed. She couldn't look at Charlie. She said, "We met at a party—you know how it happens—a tennis or a dance party." This was a story she had no business telling.

"Which was it?" said Wetherbee. "We want to picture you."

"Oh, well, then, picture us in white." She smoothed Franklin's hair off his forehead as if she were done speaking.

But Wetherbee crossed his arms across his chest and settled back in his chair ready to listen.

"The young people of Lowell were in their summer togs." She was being flip, but what else was she going to do with all of them waiting? "We'd been playing tennis at one house or another on Belvidere Hill, but then a rain storm came up, and it turned into a Tom Collins party, like the rest of them. You can imagine."

"We can? Whose house was it?" asked Wetherbee.

Standing by Franklin's highchair was too much like being on stage. She didn't like the sort of attention Wetherbee turned on her. "Charlie, you tell it. You tell it so much better." It was really his story.

Charlie frowned and shook his head, once. She knew that if he hadn't had his mouth full, he would have told them how when he saw her, he knew she was the one. Delia Barnett was going to be his bride. For him, it had been love at first sight.

Wetherbee said, "Where was this party?"

"Oh, I don't know. The Morgans', the Coopers', the Banks'. What difference would that make?"

Bess said, "Charlie was always so handsome, just like his father."

Delia maintained that meeting him had been as much a turning point in her life as meeting her had been in his. But the truth was that she didn't remember a thing about it. She flashed one of her best smiles in Charlie's direction.

Wetherbee leaned closer and said, "When you saw him, did it just hit you like lightning?" He held his lips as if he had a secret in his cheek. She began to think he knew just how much she didn't remember.

Charlie loved to tell the story of seeing her for the first time. He was really quite sentimental about the whole thing. His face would light up as he described how she looked, what she wore, how she sat swinging her long legs. Charlie knew at once that something definitive and unalterable had just happened to him. He put so much stock in it. She couldn't even remember where she'd been sitting to swing her legs like that.

She said, "Here came this skinny older boy, a man really—he was in medical school—in his tennis whites, in one of those V-necked sweaters with the red and blue piping." She supposed, she hoped, that Charlie'd had one of those awful sweaters. "He had such a hopeful bounce to his step." Looking back on that tall, thin man, she saw how sweetly he'd probably worn his prim sweater.

"But what did you feel?" asked Wetherbee, planting his elbows on the table.

His self-assuredness reminded her of the first time she'd gone to him. He hadn't been working for them for long. He'd left the usual flowers in the music room that morning. But she had been there, passed out on the couch, wearing her muskrat coat inside out—the way she liked it—fur side to skin. He'd come in with the flowers, and she imagined he stood in the doorway looking at her sleeping while he deliberated whether he should perhaps come back later. Her bare feet and calves would have been exposed, her hair tossed back on the sofa pillow, the satin lining of her coat moving as she breathed. Even though, or maybe *because*, it signaled that he'd seen her like that, he had left the flowers.

Bess and Gwen looked expectantly at her. She said, "Charlie stood out because his attention to me didn't waver for a minute." That part was true. She glanced at Charlie. He scooped his dropped napkin from the floor as if he weren't listening, but the veins at his temples stood out. She would have to smooth this over when they were alone in the car.

Wetherbee fixed her with his eyes. She saw his fine head, his craggy face, his full lips. He was magnificent, and he was manipulating her just as he had the aunts. She remembered how he'd started finding excuses to come in the house in the late afternoon, just when she expected Charlie home. She had begun to feel uneasy, as if Wetherbee could be in the house anytime, anywhere—that it was possible she'd climb out of the bath and reach for a towel and he would be there, uninvited, to hand it to her.

"Go on," he said. Had she told him she didn't remember meeting Charlie?

"After he saw me—," she faltered and felt them all waiting. Then she skated out across her own false brightness. "After he saw me, no other girl could turn his head, not even Caroline Wheelwright." Those were his words, lifted right from his story. She felt as if she had been pushed to some high place, a promontory over the sea where the wind blew past her ears, obscuring everything but her own voice, full and airy with lies, telling . . . telling whatever she thought up to tell. "When I first met him, I went around calling him Edgar and asking people if they wanted to meet my friend Edgar Rice Burroughs." She could have done that. "I was very young." Could that excuse her? "Charlie will say that he knew the moment he met me that I was his fate."

Charlie held his fork suspended over his plate. The aunts looked from her to him. He didn't let on. But the skin around his eyes tightened.

"Was that the moment you knew he was the ONE?" said Wetherbee, his focus on Delia unwavering.

She jutted her chin into the air. He'd done enough damage. When she'd told him he was no longer welcome, even as a gardener, he was fired, he had fallen silent, had sucked in the fullness of his lower lip and stared at her defiantly, as if he'd known all along that this would be the way it would happen. She'd kept her voice flat when she'd said, "I cannot trust you."

Now, she hummed a few notes, lightly, as if she were in control. "As the song says, the rest of the story," and here she sang, "ain't no one's dirty business . . ."

Gwen's milky-edged eyes locked onto Bess's. One of Bess's eyebrows rose a fraction of an inch. They agreed. Gwen reached for the water pitcher and filled Bess's glass. No matter the old money Delia had brought to the marriage, she'd never quite met their standards.

She kept singing, "How my baby treats me."

Wetherbee leaned closer, resting his chin in his hand.

After he had left her house that last time, she'd thrown a Waterford pitcher at the glass door of the music room. She had wanted him, wanted to drown in him. Was that love? Water soared out in a brilliant arc as she hurled the crystal pitcher. It hit with all the force of what hurt. Such a bright and awful shattering of glass against glass and splashing water. She'd stood in the silence afterward and thought she'd broken everything there was to break, except her marriage. She didn't know if what she had with Charlie was love, either.

Charlie had found her curled in a chair in the music room, not moving, the dark coming on, and the cool air from the garden pouring though the jagged glass of the door. He'd turned on the light and looked from her to the mess she'd made. She was puffy-eyed and ugly with crying.

"What's all this?" he'd said. He'd gone for a wastebasket. As he crouched with a dustpan and broom, the light from the sconce had fallen warmly on his face. His look seemed one of pleasure in tending to her, a contentment in providing what was needed to compensate for her weaknesses—as if in caring for her, he had won something, and that thing he did with the broom was just part of what was expected of a winner.

Now Charlie said, "Aunties, I notice you've got a bumper crop of pumpkins coming. I like the one climbing the apple tree."

Bess said, "That pumpkin wasn't our idea. That one's a volunteer."

Charlie said, "Well, I like the idea of a tree full of pumpkins." He made himself laugh heartily. "Have you seen it, Delia?"

She looked at his unnaturally animated face and couldn't answer. Why was he talking about pumpkins? Charlie had thought she'd cried with remorse for having ruined both the fine old pitcher and the door, for having lost her temper again, for having fired another gardener. Or, she had believed that until this minute. She laid her knife and fork side by side across her plate.

He went on, "The vine has gone right up that little tree, and instead of apples, they've got six-inch yellow pumpkins dangling among the branches." His look shifted from the saltcellar, to the pepper grinder, out the window, at his plate. "Dangling like ornaments, harvest baubles in an apple tree."

Delia eased her back into her chair for support. He was rescuing her. Through the wavery window, the tired lilac leaves were still. How long had he known? He strained over his plate like a growing boy, cleaning it quickly to catch up with the rest of them. Maybe he knew even back when he swept up the broken glass. Now, he swabbed up the last of his turnip with a bit of game hen and chewed energetically.

Maybe what she'd thought was satisfaction on his face as he cleaned up the glass was really victory because she'd banished Wetherbee. And if that were so, couldn't she see it as proof of his feelings for her, proof of what a good, patient man he was? She imagined feeling swamped by gratitude to Charlie. He pulled the napkin from his shirt and folded it closed on the table. How easy, to be grateful for his generosity and discretion. For his loyalty. A feeling of such ecstatic relief spread through her, reaching like the heat of a strong drink right to the tips of her fingers. They would get through this day and put it behind them.

Gwen said, "Bess thought we should rip that pumpkin vine out, but Mr. Wetherbee convinced her."

Wetherbee was looking at her. She didn't care. She set her jaw and looked back. She couldn't read what was written there, but couldn't help admiring the shape of his head, the solidity of his chest and neck. One hand lay open on the table. She followed the beautiful curve of vein, which wound from his wrist up his forearm and under the rolled cuff of his shirt. He was, perhaps, the mistake—in a string of mistakes—whose memory she would savor most. She turned away to Charlie, who was speaking. He sat squarely, upright, at ease at the head of the table. Even when she could not love herself, he could.

He smoothed the back of his head and said, "We must be going along." He patted his napkin on the table. "I want to hear no objections from you two ladies, to our skipping dessert. You know I like to get home before dark. Wetherbee," he said, rising, "Be a good man, will you, and help these ladies clear."

She and Charlie rode quietly with half a peach cake on the seat between them. When they'd left, Delia gave each of the aunts a quick peck on the cheek—which seemed more than they were ready for—and then busied herself by carrying Franklin, limp in his blanket, to the car. She had managed to avoid Wetherbee.

She untucked a corner of wax paper from the cake and pinched off a bite with her fingers. The quiet seemed to surround them then, putting a cushion between them and where they'd been. She'd been waiting for the right moment to smooth things over. She said, "I—"

But Charlie cut her off. "You're not going to speak to me now. You've said enough today. The last thing we needed was your dirty laundry aired at that table." He held the wheel with two hands. "You are not going to say a word to me until you know precisely what needs to be said." He turned to look in the sideview mirror. There was no one else on the road.

She sat stunned. She watched his chiseled profile for some softening. He faced forward as if he were driving alone. Beyond him, the telephone wires swooped down and up, from pole to pole as they passed. Past the Ouellette Bridge, onto Lakeview, past the long view of the mills along the Merrimack River. Then the crowded three-deckers one after another, as they drove through the Bleachery toward Belvidere Hill, and still Charlie didn't relax.

The aunts didn't have a clue about her and Wetherbee, but they had exchanged a look. She'd seen it. Silently, they'd agreed that she didn't measure up. She had sung at the table; she had said "ain't." She had pretended to remember things she didn't. She wasn't good enough for their darling Charlie.

Each time she'd made a mess of things, Charlie had come and cleaned up after her. Each time he'd saved her, he had gone a little beyond her. The satisfaction she'd seen in Charlie's face as he swept up the glass, and again today, had nothing to do with winning out over Wetherbee. Each time he rescued her, he affirmed that he was just that bit superior to her.

How could she not have seen? The aunts, even the aunts, knew it. It wasn't Wetherbee, but she, he'd beaten. Charlie was more capable, more generous and honest. They all knew it. The bastard was a better person, and he had only to wait a while and she would prove it again.

They pulled into their driveway, where the hard shadow of the beech trees appeared as a gaping hole between them and the house. He turned off the car, opened the door, and swiveled his feet to the pavement. His shoulders in the tweed jacket looked trim, complete, and sure. The door clicked quietly as he closed it behind him. She'd thought he would do anything for her. How smoothly he moved away through the shadows of the trees—not a motion wasted as he left her behind with Franklin.

Gumbo Limbo

June DeLisle cooled her feet in the tea-colored water of Xipal Creek while purple blossoms shaped like doll hats sifted down from high in the trees, blessing her shoulders and hair and drifting away on the slow water. For once in her life, she didn't care that she was too fat, her perm had wilted flat, and her slacks stuck at the tops of her thighs.

Behind her, the land sloped through deep layers of tree-shade, but at her feet, sun glinted off the water, making her squint. A bird glimmered on a vine. She flipped the pages of her field guide. She'd never remember all the names. Wavery light, reflecting off the water, rippled across her pale round face. A Green Kingfisher.

June didn't notice things as much as she should. She needed to learn to pay better attention. At home in Lowell, if she and Norm sat on the front porch of their second-floor apartment on Ames Street and Norm said, "Someone sure fixed that Chevy up nice," chances were that June wouldn't know a truck had gone by.

Norm would say, "What is it that takes so much concentrating?"

She didn't know.

He'd say, "That truck could have gone up your nose and you'd ask, 'What truck?'"

Leathery leaves rustled high in the trees, and a fuzzy brown fruit bounced down onto the path behind her like a clue to something. Her neck and shoulders were stiff from looking up. Of all the amazing things here, the strangest was how much she liked it. She'd never dreamed Central America was a place she, June DeLisle, would go.

At home she'd started visiting the Plum Island Wildlife Refuge. She just wanted a place to be alone, and it had a big old empty beach. In the salon where she worked, the damp and sleepy mothers yawned and compared diaper brands while she dried their hair. As she walked home, they clogged the sidewalks of Lowell's Bleachery neighborhood with brightly colored strollers and talked about C-sections like they missed them. In the three-decker where June and Norm lived, other women's lives squeezed up against hers. Kristal, upstairs, complained back and forth with Mary Ann, downstairs, about leaky boobs, while their babies howled. (In high school, when June thought she was pregnant they'd been so scared they got married. Afterward, when it turned out she wasn't, Norm decided he didn't want kids.)

Norm, being a trucker, could relate to her wanting to get away. But she hadn't ever been able to explain well enough about seeing the bird in the refuge parking lot. She saw a bird, and it started a change in her. It sounded dumb, she knew. She tried to tell him how she was standing by the car, not really wanting to get back to work, feeling like she had no excuse for taking up air, when something moved in the poison ivy by the bumper. A tiny yellow bird with a black mask peeked out at her. She tried to get Norm to understand it wasn't just that the bird was cute. "Its mask was black as a thief's." Something that little and perfect lived a whole life in secret, and she'd never thought anything of it.

"I hear the birds singing in springtime," he said. "What's the big deal?" He was just trying to stop her from getting too soapy.

But that bird had come especially to be noticed by her. She'd never really thought about how, even as close as outside her window, other living things were born, and ate their meals, and slept, and had their babies, and died. All sorts of lives ran right alongside the one she was living. June began wanting to look around.

She'd been back to Plum Island again and again. Without mentioning it to Norm, she saved for the binoculars in the gift shop by setting aside a few of her tips each week. She doubted she was noticing the important things, but with binoculars she could sit at the base of a dune and feel like she was right in the choppy swells with the cormorants and ducks.

When Norm saw how she'd spent their money, he said, "Peewee, can you name one, just *one* person we know who wants to go looking at *birds*?"

A leaf fell onto the water. She folded it and set it sailing. A bird, low in the bushes, where she couldn't see, sang ♪ ♫ ♫. Her hands smelled like pumpkin pie.

She'd bought the raffle ticket for a trip to Belize from the refuge attendant. The brochure showed Xipal Lodge, with its thatched-roof cabanas, "nestled in the wintering grounds of New England's favorite birds." The trip for two was all expenses paid. She'd never won a thing before and thought there'd been a mistake.

Allspice. That was the smell on her hands. A howler monkey started up like a sudden wind, and stopped. They woke her before dawn with their weird alarm, just like the brochure said. They lived in the high ridges by the Guatemalan border. The brochure said jaguars lived in this forest, too.

Norm had said, "Do the other girls from the salon do this kind of thing? Can you see Dawn with a bird book? Stella's like me, she'd drive a foreign-made car before she'd sling a pair of binoculars around her neck." Stella was June's boss at A Cut Above. Norm said the only thing it was above was the Phoenix Luncheonette, downstairs.

June breathed smells of sweetness and rot, and tugged at her damp shirt. The slope rose behind her, trunks, roots, and dirt in shadow. Across the creek, beyond the bright leafy thickets, the land swept up steeply again. There was no one here but her. She surprised herself with the idea that she could take her clothes off and swim. She couldn't think of another time in her whole life when that had been possible. She wiped the sweat off her upper lip and noticed a pool farther up the creek that looked a little deeper.

She stepped back onto the path trying to imagine herself telling Norm at lunch, "I swam naked," but that was too wild sounding. She tried, "I went skinny dipping," and then settled on, "I was so hot, I took my clothes off and waded into the water." She probably wouldn't mention it at all.

When she'd gotten the airplane tickets and the voucher for Xipal Lodge, Norm set his mind on selling them. He'd always wanted to go snowmobiling in the Connecticut Lakes. She told him no one else could use the tickets. They had to be the ones to go. She didn't say how much she wanted to.

He told her to call the wildlife refuge and ask. She put it off. He said, "How many times do I have to ask you?" Another time, he said, "Do I have to make the call myself?" She said, "You can call, but it says the rules right here." She read them aloud to him, carefully pronouncing the part about nontransferable. He said, "I'm going to call," and she said, "Go ahead. I'm going to Xipal Lodge." That gave her a start, saying that. As if she had given her own self a shot in the arm and jumped when the needle went in. He swiveled his head at her. She kept her eyes down. He took his beer to the TV.

Had she meant she would go without him? When she was at work and looking at the toucans in the brochure, she imagined going even if he didn't. But walking up the block from the salon on Central Street, breathing the inescapable smell of the river, and climbing the stairs to their apartment, she wished there were some way she *could* go, and by the time she reached the second-floor landing and unlocked their apartment door, she was hoping that he would either say they were going or they weren't.

She put the tickets on the corkboard by the phone. A few weeks before they were supposed to leave, he said, "We couldn't go even if we wanted to. We don't have passports." She fiddled with the tassels on the couch and turned up the TV.

"They're all ready, except for your picture and your signature. We just have to get them to the post office." She'd filled out the forms with her heart fluttering and banging around (as it was now), her hands sweating like the first time she unrolled a perm. "They said we show them at the airport in Boston and again when we get there."

He stared at her, which was the way he usually won. Then the doorbell rang. She pulled herself up to answer it. He followed her, stuck on what she'd just said, his face like a fist.

His friend Paul stood at the door. Big slovenly Paul, with his baseball cap on backward, said, "Hey, my truck's idling rough. I wondered if you could take a look under the hood."

Norm said, "Sure." He grabbed June's arm. "You won't mind if I just . . ."—he twisted it behind her back—". . . finish up a little chat I've been having with my wife." They laughed, and June said, "Ow, ow, ow."

Norm said, "Say, 'I was only kidding about passports.'" He kept twisting until she was bent almost to the floor and panted out, "Kidding."

After the men went downstairs, June swept their second-story porch and put her feet up. Without peeking through the railing, she knew Norm would have his sleeves rolled up and his hands busy in the engine. One of her favorite ways to see him was leaning over a truck like it was twenty years ago and they were still in high school. He'd be holding his cigarette in his teeth with smoke curling up into his eyes, making him squint while he talked.

He was telling Paul that just because she'd won a raffle, she thought they were going to a jungle. "Like *I* would ever go to a fucking jungle," he said. "She's got this thing about birds."

June shrank in her chair.

"Maybe she's going through the change early," Paul said. "Patti started collecting figurines last year. Now they're everywhere. Little porcelain statues; big-time mood swings. She barely leaves the house. But you: Your wife wins a trip for two, and you're not going? Is it a resort, or what?"

There was a tapping noise. Norm said, "Take that clamp off. When I say tarantulas big as pie plates, does that say resort to you?"

"You pussy."

There was quiet.

Then Norm said, "You got a Phillips?"

June leaned her head against the railing and closed her eyes. *"Please Paul,"* she thought, *"if you tell him, he'll listen."*

She heard Paul rummaging in his toolbox. He said, "You gotta go, chicken shit. You stay home, I'm buying you your own set of figurines."

～

The head of a tiny, iridescent bird lay in June's path, as if it were buried up to its neck. The head—a brilliant blue, no bigger than a beetle—was all by itself. June pushed at it with a fingernail to make sure. How did a bird get its head cut clean off? It seemed so tidy and over with, lost, like a feather or a tooth. Its eyes hadn't dimmed. She looked into the tree above her, not knowing what she'd see. Empty branches. She was flipping to the blue pages in her guidebook when the leaves just across the creek gathered into the shape of a face, a dappled face.

June fumbled *The Birds of Central America*. She caught it, but when she looked up again, the face was gone. A cicada started up loudly. The tea-colored creek gurgled on as if nothing had changed. She tried to think what to do that wouldn't be stupid. She couldn't run very fast, especially uphill. She focused on the spot where the face had been.

"Are you alone?" A girl, maybe twenty, with an American accent— and with a lot of black hair falling from a messy ponytail—stepped partway into the light across the creek. Here was the sort of face June had always wished she had, high cheekbones, straight little nose. But the girl's eyes were scared mean like the dog tied in the alley, back home. She was sickly pale. Leaves and plant bits stuck in her hair. "I asked if you're alone," the girl said, pushing her voice hard against the words.

June wished she wasn't. "The others are up there," she said.

The girl drew back into the leaves like a snake. "Where?"

June pointed with her book. "Xipal Lodge."

"But *here*?" she insisted. "Tell me."

June wished Norm was nearby—instead of at the bar. She shook her head.

This girl looked fit, like she could move fast. She searched the dark rise on June's side of the creek, then yanked off her sandals and pushed suddenly through the water toward her. June held still. She didn't breathe.

The girl didn't have anything in her hands but her shoes. She stopped halfway across and squinted, scanning up and down the creek bed. "I've hurt my foot and I'm not even out of Guatemala."

She sounded so sure that June, doubting what she knew, said, "This is Belize, I think."

The stranger looked June up and down, and dismissed her, the way most people did. June began to relax. The girl swished her foot in the creek. "Not that a border will stop them," she said wryly, as if she were making a wisecrack. June didn't get it. Stop who? Changes passed over the girl's face so fast. Norm would slide his hand up and down in front of his face changing it from a smile to a frown to an angry jack-o'-lantern so convincingly that she couldn't tell the difference between anger and the look of anger.

The girl wore a red-and-blue cotton top like the natives, but with khaki pants. She pulled her wet pant-leg up her calf. "Looks infected," she said, lifting a swollen foot out of the water. "What a nuisance."

If someone as pushy and abrupt came into the salon, June would get busy with something else, sorting curlers or cleaning brushes. Her boss, Stella, would handle the situation.

The girl's hands shook as she cupped water to cool her arms and neck. She dunked her tangled hair and let it drip down her face without blinking or wiping her eyes. Maybe she was making a show of how hot she felt. "I'm so thirsty. Have you got anything?" the girl asked.

June should have had water with her. If she'd thought about it before—they *had* warned her about dehydration in this heat. She felt ashamed. "They've got filtered water up at the lodge," she said, her face turning red.

"Lot of good that'll do me."

"I'm sorry." Even as she spoke, June knew she was being dopey. "I could get you some."

The girl said, "You'll have to. I can't go up there."

"The lodge isn't far at all."

"It wouldn't matter if it were behind that tree." The look the strange girl gave June could have peeled skin. "When you get me something to drink, you can't tell anyone you saw me. No one. If you do, what happens will be your fault."

June's eyes stung. "Who's after you?"

The girl strained forward as if she were going to cry. Or throw up. Then she pushed her hair out of her face, which changed again, to a mask of impatience. She said, "No one you know. Bring some food, too. Hurry."

Waiting for the dining room doors to open, June sat by the postcard rack, her heart churning so hard she could hear it. Her knees bounced. What would Norm do? The chalkboard by the door said chili for lunch. How could she carry chili to the creek? Should she even try? How did she know the girl wasn't some sort of criminal?

She distracted herself by looking at the postcards. She'd sent the one with the yellow border and insets of jungle animals to Stella and Dawn at the salon. The close-up of a jaguar kept catching her eye. She would like to tell someone about how she'd felt just before she'd seen the girl—how good and alive she felt breathing the soft air, standing quietly in the creek with the petals blessing her, the birds singing, and the sunlight glinting off the big green leaves. She wished someone could have known her, really known what she was like, right then in her life.

She would maybe address the card with the toucan holding a passion fruit to Norm, who was taking his vacation in the bar.

Dear Norm, I think allspice grows here. I folded a leaf and then my hands smelled like pumpkin pie. I saw a coatimundi today with a long raccoon-y tail. Seeing it, I felt like someone handed me a present. Like someone said, Here is this for you to see that you couldn't have imagined in a million years. It jumped down from a gumbo-limbo tree, and bounced away like a monkey. They call gumbo-limbo "tourist" trees because they peel pink like you do in the sun. What a place this is! Love, Peewee

P.S. If you would only open your eyes and look around.

She couldn't say that.

Dear Norm, Wish you were here. Your wife, June DeLisle.

He could get away with something like that, but not June. He would be too hurt. In the days after she'd said or done something wrong—when he wouldn't talk to her—his stony, dark-eyed stare would show her all the meanness of the world. In his eyes she would see a hard, empty place. And he would remind her that he was all that protected her from it.

Dear Norm, You'd love lunch. The chili smells really good, better than that Boca Grande place you like on Route 3. Miss you. Love, Peewee

She took a last look at the card of a beautiful sunset over the tropical forest.

Dear Norm, I can't tell you about this, but I'm supposed to get supplies for

someone who came out of nowhere this morning. She is running away from Gua-
temala. I can't tell if she has done something awful, or if something awful hap-
pened to her. She won't come near the lodge. She has an infected foot and shaky
hands. I can guess what you'd say about this. Love, June

He'd say, *Keep your nose out of it.*

The round tables and squat wooden chairs, the slim brown waitresses in their gingham dresses and aprons, the air, the people eating, the lazy wooden fans hanging from the ceiling—everything under the octagonal roof of the dining cabana—flexed weirdly, along with her gushing pulse. A German couple sat at her table.

Helga, who had worked up a good sweat touring the Mayan ruins with her small husband, said, "Those Guatemalans dug up everything." June didn't know what to say. She'd had to teach herself how to chat with her clients so she wouldn't lose her job. She still had overeager moments, like when an ex-con came in for a trim and told her he'd killed a man and she asked, all chirpy, "Oh, and who did you kill?"

Helga said, "In the burial grounds, robbers shoveled almost every thing to ruins."

June said, "Oh my." She was thinking that just because the girl at the creek looked bad, didn't mean she was bad. She was strangely bossy and afraid and confident and dirty. What if June went back and met up with whoever was after the girl? But what if June didn't take her any supplies? What then? June screwed up the courage to slip a roll into her sleeve. Usually, she couldn't have stood the awful feeling of sneaking something. Blood whooshed in and out of her head. She didn't know what she was doing.

Norm sprawled on their bed under the ceiling fan. Over time, his shape had been molded by the seat of his rig: big arms and chest, solid round belly, flat butt, and flat feet. With his eyes closed he looked locked away. But his mouth hung slack and soft as a little boy's. She watched him just long enough to make sure that the flowers on his Hawaiian shirt rose and fell with a regular sleeping breath. He'd said Belizean beer was mostly water, but he spent a good chunk of each day sleeping it off.

June hovered over their suitcase, trying to decide what to do. Norm would say, *It's none of your business what these people do.* And that would be that. But she was humming with a strange energy, as if her body contained all that she'd seen that day. She felt jangly and full-up. She looked for the Band-Aids and first-aid cream she'd packed in a ziplock bag. How was she supposed to carry water? She didn't know what to put it in. How much should she try to take? *Quit dithering.* She found a couple of Wash'n Dris and unzipped her beauty case.

"Peewee, that you?" Norm rolled over.

She held still, hoping he'd go back to sleep.

He said, "Come here, you. Where you been?"

She sat on the edge of the bed and tried to smooth down the bed-spread, which bloomed all over with huge blue orchids. The thrumming was in her ears now.

Norm's big cheek was creased and pink from the pillow. He sat up. "I was hoping you'd come along." He could be so sweet when he'd just woken up.

He put his meaty arms around her from behind, just the way she usually loved him to hold her. Ever since he'd said they were coming on this trip, he'd sulked and hadn't touched her at all. Now his hand floated toward her breasts.

She tried to turn away, but he held her. She gave a little trill of a dismissing laugh, but he flicked open the buttons of her shirt.

"Norm."

He pulled her shirt, like damp petals, away from her sticky skin.

"Not now." She couldn't tell him why. "Please." Sometimes she felt so sad for him.

She clenched her teeth and tried again to turn from him but he got under her bra. He could be so tender. She saw herself, her many selves, over the years, saying *yes* to him, a line-up of all the Junes, stretching the whole way back to high school, *yes*, *yes*, like the nearly identical stuffed bird skins on their backs in the display case at the wildlife refuge—lined up one after another, *yes*, cotton batting showing through the eye slits.

"No."

"What better thing have you got to do?" he said into her neck.

She couldn't say. All that she couldn't say hummed inside her. She edged a little away from him, trying to think. "I said we had some," she held up the ziplock bag of first-aid cream. "Someone needs it."

He kept her where she was. He touched her ear, just there, with his tongue.

Her ear—the rim of the thrumming she held inside—the very edge that kept back the rest. Just there, with his tongue.

She let the ziplock bag go, and rolled toward him. She pushed herself and everything she felt into his hands.

He cracked her open like a big, soft egg.

June dreamt a dream more real than her life. In it, she rides a bus that's barely a bus anymore, stripped-down, beat-up, the kind that carries nothing but natives and trouble. Dusty palm leaves, hanging down, scrape the bus. The girl is with her. Her name is Lacy, the name June always thought she'd name a baby. But the girl is not a baby. She is limp and feverish on the seat next to June. The bus has stopped. June has to lift her. She takes Lacy's belt like a handle, bracing her with her hip, amazed at her own strength, not sure the driver will stop long enough to let them off. They have luggage. A backpack and a duffel bag, which June also lifts. Lacy's sandaled feet, her white hands, trail down the steps and through the dirt of the road. June pushes the knapsack with her foot and eases Lacy onto it as if it were a pillow. Lacy's black ponytail dips in the dust. The sky's a hammering blue. June is looking for the Red Cross. She sees two goats. A rusted out Coca-Cola sign. She is thinking like someone who knows how to make things happen.

The jungle has opened out enough for a clump of tiny, colorful houses painted like the midway at the Topsfield Fair. Lacy's chest heaves; she turns to the side and vomits in the road. It's not just her foot, or her streaky leg, but Lacy, all of her, that's sick. June wipes Lacy's mouth with a mashed-up tissue she must have found in her pocket. Lacy's foot is so swollen, it's going to bust her sandal straps. June undoes the buckles. She knocks on a door. Everything smells like smoke.

A boy, quick as a wren, looks at her with gold eyes. Every minute counts.

"Where's the doctor?" she asks.

The boy, who can't be more than ten or eleven, disappears into the house.

Was that the last she'll see of help? She's sweating and wipes her face with the back of her hand. A lot of good that does. She pulls out her shirt-tail and wipes her face on that.

The boy is back, standing shyly behind a bigger boy, who is almost old enough to shave. The big one says, "You need a truck?"

She can't tell if he speaks English or can just say the one phrase. She says, "A doctor. But first water."

The big one says something in Spanish to the littler one and points at a barrel by the downspout. June doesn't remember what the travel book said about rainwater; could you drink it? She says, "No, wait. Coke. Do you have any Coca-Cola?"

The little boy stops and looks at the bigger one, who shakes his head. The little one fills a dipper of water and carries it, dripping, to June.

She would like to drink it all herself, right there, parasites and all, just drink it down, she is so thirsty, but she cradles it over to Lacy, with the boys following. She lifts Lacy's head. What if the water makes her sicker? Squatting there with the two boys, June closes her eyes. Dehydration or parasites? She says, "I'll give you a dollar for a Coke." She pulls out a U.S. bill. "Then you get the doctor, as fast as you can." The big kid says, "Okay," takes her money, and does what she says.

June wakes gritty-eyed and thirsty, too hot under the flowered bedspread. Norm snores on his back. How could she have fallen asleep?

Her slacks are around her ankles. She pulls them up and buttons her shirt. She knows what she has to do. She slides off the bed carefully. She finds a plastic mug with a snap-lid that says *Xipal Lodge* and fills it with filtered water, drinks it and fills it again, watching her hands work. A larger bottle would be better, but there isn't one.

The light is different on the path. She doesn't know what time it is. A pale animal like a tall guinea pig lopes away in the shadows. An Agouti.

The girl's hiding place was a good one. It would be hard for anyone to see her between the buttress roots of the strangler fig trees that are smothering the gumbo-limbos along the creek. June's sure the girl is waiting.

She finds the tiny bird head. Blue Bunting. This is the place. She pretends to be looking for birds. Through her binoculars, she scans the undergrowth across the creek. She can't see the girl. Good, then no one else could either. Her pulse beats in her forehead. The woods look undisturbed. Maybe they got lucky and no one followed the girl from Guatemala. June crosses the creek, just steps right in, saturating her sneakers and her thin socks. The girl is not where she left her. Rather than calling out, June whistles ♪ ♫ ♫. It is just another noise, come and gone. She hears birds moving through the canopy above her, but can't see them.

She sits where the girl was supposed to wait, between the tree roots. If she waits a while, the girl will show up. June balances the mug in the dirt. She will convince the girl to trust her, to come up to the lodge.

A line of ants, carrying bits of green leaves like banners, flows into a hole in the hard, sandy ground by the mug.

June imagines hiding the girl in the closet of their cabana. She will get help for her. Maybe the van driver could take her somewhere safe. June will know what to do when the time comes.

It can't be that she is too late. It just can't.

June rummages in her Red Sox fanny pack, checking her supplies—two flattened dinner rolls, the ziplock bags—and comes upon a plastic rain bonnet folded like an accordion in its purple wrapper. She'd packed it in Lowell, planning ahead for her idea of a rain forest. The wrapper shows an older woman with glamorous lips wearing the bonnet to protect her permanent. June touches the sweaty, bleached frizz on her own head. Stella had done it fresh for her before she left home.

Fingering the folded bonnet, June pictures the dusty canisters of rain bonnets and combs on the counter at the salon. She can see herself there, fat in her pink and turquoise smock, her matching stretch pants, dusting the counter, keeping quiet, while Stella tells stories to make her clients laugh. June will sweep, clear all the cut hair from the floor beneath Stella's chair, then she'll sort the curlers by size, refold the pile of smocks, and refresh the comb-cleaning solution at each chair. She rests her back where the fig bark drapes like elephant skin over the peeling pink of the gumbo-limbo tree it is killing slowly. The creek water looks black. Purple blossoms are still floating slowly downstream. She watches them go on their way, bobbing carelessly, easily, as if nothing matters, as if it weren't true that everything depends on the girl coming back.

Smoke

THE NEXT MORNING, THE LITTLE BOY, FRANKLIN BURROUGHS, STOOD VERY still outside his parents' bedroom. He could hear them breathing. His father, Charlie, had his hand hanging over the edge of his bed, limp as the things in the butcher's window. Franklin could see his mother's black hair sticking up on her pillow. He wanted her, but he knew he must be quiet until the Hub Mills' whistle blew far away down the hill. The rule was to be very quiet until he heard the whistle. His mother told him when his father was a little boy just like him and spent summers in this house, there were ten whistles. All the mills but his grandfather's were gone now. Franklin wanted his father to go to work today, but Mr. Kinsley's truck with the sliding door that roared shut had just delivered eggs. The eggs were waiting in the damp carton on the back stoop. Which meant it was the day Daddy stayed home and the boy did things wrong, and his father said a crybaby was no son of his.

The sun made rainbows on the edge of the closet mirror. He wished he could show that to his mother. Her sewing table was still all tidied up from yesterday when she got ready for the party for people from Daddy's work. She'd rushed and rushed until the laundry pile wasn't there. She frowned and held pins between her lips while she fixed her dress. All day, she'd been cross with him, except when he asked nicely and she let him lick the cake beaters.

Now, sleeping, she whistled, "*Shhh. Shhh.*" Franklin was trying to be quiet, but his mouth was filling up with spit. He knew how much noise it would make if he swallowed, and he had to be a good boy. His father called it saliva and said Delia, the boy's mother, should teach him the proper words for things. He needed to swallow it. A friend of his mother's called it drool. His throat started to close, but he stopped it just in time. Babies drool. His mouth kept filling. He couldn't help it. It was like crying, like tears coming when he knew they shouldn't. Spit kept coming. What should he do? How could he stop? His throat kept trying to do it. Then he had to. He shut his eyes tight. He swallowed. It was like thunder in his ears.

He waited. He opened his eyes. His father's hanging-down hand didn't move. The hallway where he stood seemed big and full of air.

He would play with his farm. He kept his rubber farm animals in their fences. The horses stuck their heads over. Grown-ups were always asking what chickens and pigs and cows say. Everyone knows where milk comes from. On their TV, Captain Kangaroo and Mr. Green Jeans sang, "The Farmer takes a wife, the wife takes a child, the child takes a nurse, and the mouse takes the cheese." The boy could sing "Old MacDonald," too, but his mother said the part about taking a nurse would never happen.

His farm was in the music room. He picked his legs up high to walk so that the bottoms of his pajama feet would not be noisy on the wood. His mother's high heels, the peach-colored ones she'd worn to the party, pointed at one another in the hallway.

He'd forgotten the music room was all different. His farm was put away. Couches and chairs were pushed against the walls. Dirty glasses, with napkins under them, lined up on the piano and the windowsills.

Last night, when he woke in his room, around him had been black dark like a cave, except the streetlight shone at his eyes. The whiteness of it curved and wobbled when he cried, which made him shut his eyes and cry louder. His mother didn't come.

His father did. He smelled the way he did when he was ready to go to work. But it was night, and laughter came up the stairs from the music room. His father's arms were stronger than his mother's, but the boy was afraid he might fall because he wasn't used to them. When his father carried him down to the party, he was as high up as on a seesaw. The lights were too bright and reflected in the people's drink glasses.

They said, "There's the little fella," and "Are you shy, sport?" and looked at him, so he kept his eyes closed while his father said, "Shake hands, boy," and pulled his hands away from his face, until a lady's voice said, "Let him be, Charlie; the little darling just woke up." He peeked at the stranger. She said, "Where did you get those big blue eyes?" She had lips the color of his fire engine, and they smiled at him. His father called the lady Rosalee. Franklin got the same special feeling looking at her that he got when his mother let him play with the jewelry she kept in her special wooden music box with the red stripe.

His mother came, looking very pretty in her sparkly earrings, smiling at everyone. Didn't she see him? She leaned close to his father, not smiling anymore, and whispered in his father's ear, "Maybe if you could take your eyes off the nursing staff long enough to announce that dinner's ready, I could serve."

His mother's apron was tied in a bow on her back. She went fast, then ducked into the kitchen.

His father carried him into the dining room, where everyone was talking at once like in Stella's beauty parlor, where sometimes his mother took him with her. Then everyone sat down. The candles were lit. From his father's lap, he watched his mother bring food, getting everything the people wanted at the long table. She went quick as a bunny and looked fancy. With the oven mitt, she patted the arm of the doctor with no hair who was Daddy's boss. Her earrings sparkled like little stars next to her neck.

Rosalee put her arms out. "Can Franklin sit on my lap?" Her dress was stiff. She had a charm bracelet just like his mother's. It had a shamrock, and a Valentine heart hit by an arrow, and a baby horse sleeping, but Rosalee's had spurs. The sharp wheels went around. He twirled them. If he pressed his finger hard, it would bleed.

His mother gave Rosalee a plate and said, "You shouldn't have to do that."

Rosalee said, "It's a treat for me."

His mother said to his father, "He ought to be in bed."

His father said, "Delia: the new voice of moderation."

Rosalee smelled like flowers. The people at the other end of the table seemed far away. Except for his mother in her dress like peach ice cream, they wore dark grown-ups' colors. His daddy's boss was boss of the table, too. He talked and they all looked at him.

When Rosalee was finished eating, she let Franklin play with her fork. He made her laugh, scooping nothing wildly into his mouth from the empty plate and saying yum. He did it again and again, until his father said that was enough and pulled him into his lap, but it was okay, he wasn't really angry. His father got busy taking a drink like always. His mother stood at her place down the table and said, "It is wonderful to finally have you in our home. Here's to a smooth and happy year at the hospital." The boss said thank you. Then his mother carried plates into the kitchen. The laughing got as loud as yelling.

Rosalee said quietly, "If I'd known she was so gracious, I never would have come."

His father leaned his scratchy jacket closer to him. "I wanted you." The boy thought it would be all right to take his father's glasses out of his jacket pocket and try them on. His father said, "Do still." His hand blocked the glasses from sliding out, then didn't. The boy put the glasses on. Everything got swimmy, swirly.

Rosalee laughed at him again, and said, "Aren't you a wise owl? Look at the little professor."

"I doubt it. Not that one." Was Daddy whining? His nose hairs were bigger than usual through the glasses. He said, "I don't think we're looking at any future M.D."

Franklin turned to Rosalee and said, "A,B,C. L,M,N,O." Rosalee's face looked as wavy as when he saw himself in the oven door. She said, "Underneath the bowtie and formalities, how obnoxious is your father, really?"

His father grinned, holding a cigarette in his teeth. His father's eyes were brown.

Rosalee said, "You know I don't like that. When are you going to quit?"

His father lit it. "When you don't think I look like Cary Grant anymore."

Sudden laughter burst at the other end of the table. The man next to Rosalee turned around toward her to say, "The boss is really somethin', huh?"

She nodded. The man turned away again.

His father moved his leg up and down by Rosalee's under the table so that the boy wobbled in his lap. Franklin started to sing, "This is the way the farmer rides," but no one else did. He heard his mother whipping cream in the kitchen. She would be leaning against the counter, looking out the window, and making her hand go very fast around.

The boss boomed, "Hubert Humphrey? Are you *kidding*?"

Then came the part Franklin did wrong. His father held his cigarette near him and asked if he wanted a drag.

Rosalee said, "No. Don't," while his father said, "Put your mouth around it." His father put the Band-Aid-colored end in Franklin's mouth. He was close up to his father's smell.

The boy put his fingers the way he saw Daddy do it, which made his father laugh. So he waved it around, putting it in his mouth and pulling it out.

"Not like your mother," his father said. "You're a limp-wristed little bastard."

Franklin knew he'd disappointed Rosalee, because she slumped back in her chair. She threw her napkin on the table and didn't look at him anymore. He wanted her to. He wanted her to say more things about him.

"Watch this, Rosebud." His father was very jolly then, telling the boy, "Breathe in."

Franklin watched Rosalee frowning and tried to suck in as his father showed him, but that's when he felt fire in his stomach. He coughed and coughed until he was crying. He couldn't do it right, and it hurt. The people in the crowded room got blurry. Rosalee stood over him, saying, "Look what you've done. What is wrong with you?" Then his mother whisked him, dizzy in her warm arms, away from Rosalee and his father, and back to bed.

In one of the used glasses on the windowsill, there was a slice of orange. When his mother had work to do in the kitchen and he mustn't get in her hair, he watched from the doorway. One time when she took out an ice tray and lifted a can of mandarin slices from the refrigerator door rack, she said maybe it would be all right if he had one. She squatted on the floor and fished with two fingers in the syrupy can until she caught one. She showed him how to tilt his head back to bite it. Her shiny hair fanned out on her shoulders.

The slice tasted cold, not like fruit, partly sweet and rubbery. It squirted in his mouth. She said there was nothing like that special kind of orange in a whiskey sour. He could reach this one in the glass, he thought.

He got it. But the glass tipped off the piano. He watched while it didn't break. The thump wasn't too noisy, but the white rug was dark wet with a spill that smelled like Bactine.

He knew what to do. He'd seen his mother do it whenever he spilled. He spread the rumpled napkin on top of the stain. Then he stepped on it. This was how to blot it up. It would be okay. The napkin stuck to his pajama feet and shredded. Maybe he did it wrong. He rubbed it off on the rug and got another napkin from under another glass. He blotted some more. The wet napkin bits spread around on the stain. Sometimes when he had been clumsy and was crying, his mother would press one shoe then the other, then both fast, so it might have been a dance if she had been happy. He wouldn't worry now. He tried doing a little blotting dance and wondered if she would like to see him cleaning up, if she would think he was very clever making everything all right. He spread another napkin on top of all the spill and the napkin crumbs and shreds. He made it tidy with the clean napkin on top.

He needed to see if she was awake. He went upstairs and remembered to pick his feet up high in the hallway after the rug ended. In the doorway, he tried clearing his throat the way his father did. Then, remembering how his throat had hurt with smoke, he coughed, but just a little, pretty softly. So only his mother would hear.

Last night, when he was sad and crying, his mother, in her slippery dress, put him quickly to bed. "Shush up," she said. With her hand on the doorknob, she listened to him snuffling and said, "He's right about you, isn't he?" and then she shut the door.

Now, he coughed a bit louder, and waited. Nothing changed. He stood by the wallpaper with the fuzzy pattern he mustn't touch. There was a patch of sunlight on the floor. He stood waiting in the big empty hallway that reached all the way from his room to the stairs. He looked at his mother with her hair clumped up against the pillow. He wished he could touch it, wished she would lift her head and smile at him with her earrings sparkling, the way she had at his father's boss. He coughed again, a lot louder. But nothing changed at all.

Next to him on the wooden floor, his mother's high heels still pointed at one another. He thought he might want to try them on. He might just put on her beautiful, peach-colored shoes and make the spiky heels *clap clap clap clap clap* CLAP CLAP CLAP CLAP CLAP away down the hall.

Another Way to Make Cleopatra Cry

WE DIDN'T NOTICE WHEN MY BIG SISTER, CLEOPATRA, LEFT DAWN'S PURSE on top of the Chevette. Dawn yelled at Dooley, her own darling son, to get in his car seat, she didn't give a hoot where he'd left his shoe; we had to get to the store. I flicked the Hardee's wrappers off the backseat onto the floor with the old girlie magazines and a Cheeto that had died in the corner. Dawn shook her daisy blond hair. She'd just lost another job; this one at A Cut Above, the salon where she said she'd stick. She wrinkled her nose and said she'd had it with our daddy. What did he think he was doing, dropping three useless kids in her lap, and her life's sun not even up over the hill? This was the exact afternoon when she was going to haul herself out of this dump of a city for once and good and all and make sure our daddy, who'd been gone for days, didn't follow along after, like the goat he was. She was going to get him tethered if she had to. (We didn't know it then, but the state had taken care of that. Daddy was being held in Concord for beating up the owner of the Pump 'n' Pantry gas station/convenience store.)

No one wanted Dawn going anywhere, but that's not why her purse got left on the car. Cleopatra was balancing Dawn's open Coke in one hand and holding the door with the other, when Dawn jumped in and plunked her foot on the go-pedal like she could get away right then, so Cleopatra had no choice but to leap, spill Coke, and shut the door, all in one swoop. Cleopatra sometimes forgot stuff, but even if she'd remembered Dawn's purse, how could she have grabbed it? She wasn't even ten yet. I was barely eight. Dawn wheeled left onto the Lowell Connector, *p-voom*, with a little lift-off thrown in as she passed the Road House next door. The purse should have Frisbeed off the back and landed in that dirt-bath of a parking space. But it didn't.

I know because we looked. After we'd been to Clint's Mart—where, without the purse, we couldn't buy the salt off the back of a potato chip—and back home again, Dawn said, "How in a two-timed, toss-off of a life am I going to do ANYTHING NOW? And how could anyone, any one woman, be as crazy as your mother must've been, to name a scrawny-armed, moth-bitten child Cleopatra? Doesn't everyone know Cleopatra was beautiful and had black hair?" Dawn said this because she knew it was the one and only thing that could make Cleopatra cry. Dawn was crying mad herself, pink, like we couldn't see her standing there in her clappy-flap heels and T-shirt. "You shit-for-dirt jack-licks get out there and don't come back until you've found my bag, that, or else grown up. That means you, Kaylene."

If the screen door had known how to shut right it would've slammed. Through it, we could see her hair floating around her head like foam.

Dooley, who was three, clomped along after us with his one shoe. He wasn't our real brother because Dawn wasn't our real mother. He dragged a faded plastic boat on a string, following us up and down the two-lane that hooked the truck stop to Route 3. He was as dust-plastered as his boat, with streaks on his cheeks and scabs on his knees. We went back and forth past the Road House, where the bikers stood around in what Dawn called their toad-collared leathers, blowing smoke over the tops of their precious Harleys and scuffing black boots in the pock-marked side yard.

We eyeballed every stalk of ragweed, every yellow rag of whipping-by grass, every highway dividing post, like it was the one that had grabbed Dawn's life's work of a purse. Trucks kickballed the air past us, so we squeezed our faces shut and plugged our ears. We wore our bathing suits for clothes and pajamas, both—so later, when we were falling-down tired, we'd pick blown road-sand out of our bellybuttons. Trailing ourselves up and down along the edge of the highway connector, we couldn't get how Dawn's classy bag—not gotten at just any Wal-Mart, "you snowball brains"—could be swallowed up by pavement. It was gone, with her driver's license and her ciggies and her matches, the food stamps and her gold hoop earrings, and, worst of all, her money, her taking-off money, and "don't you forget it."

We were about on our twelfth trip past the hog-riding porkers with their bellies and their bacon-greased ponytails when one came parading out at us. He was giant. He had a tattoo as big as Dooley on his arm, and we weren't sure about the face he was making.

I remember seeing just how far away our house was. Dawn wasn't anywhere, not with her floaty hair and her fast mouth. The plastic she'd stapled around the house bottom, to keep the wind out, flapped like a wing of roadkill. That plastic, and the siding, and the yard dirt were all the same say-nothing color, and the windows gave us no clues. So I stuck my hip out and my lip out like I'd seen Dawn do to Daddy, and I flipped that big leatherette the bird.

He looked at me with his firepoker eyeballs and said, "That's real fetching." Then he asked Cleopatra, polite as a pretty-please, "You lost something?"

Doolcy couldn't talk, and we knew better. Cleopatra's blue eyes squinted up fish-shaped, and she shook her dirty-blond head. But before we could shake-a-shimmy, the fire-breather picked Dooley up like a daddy and stole him across the yard of that hog heaven. He had Dooley up on his chest like a bitty kitty of a mouse killer, and Dooley looked like he liked it.

I went after him, but I couldn't bite through because hog slipper had leather from the east to the west of his leg, and he flipped his cigarette onto the ground and plucked me up by my shoulder. He dangled me up there like a monkey and said, "Don't you want to sit on one of them bikes?"

There wasn't a whole lot I could do, and Cleopatra got all dishy-faced with yeses, so I guessed we were going to. He took about two steps, and we were there. The rest of the creaky-leather boogers backed up their circle to make room for him. They laughed at him and said, "What do you want with pets?"

The motorcycles on their kickstands sure did gleam. There was fire painted all over one, and the pipes were polished to a hoo-hah. Dangle-man set me down on the very one I bet blurted me awake in the night when my daddy fucked Dawn against the wall, and his face blinked up yellow in the glow from the TRUCK STOP sign. Dooley had his own hog-cycle; him and his boat rode a black one. But Cleopatra made like she'd found a new true daddy who wouldn't go and use her teeth to open his beer bottles. She wriggled like the puppy we used to have when we lived in the leftover motel, and slithered over Harley-Hog like she didn't care if she ever found Dawn's purse.

Next to our house, the trashcans spilled over into the weeds by the fence. My bicycle, which was also Cleopatra's, laid right where I'd left it after the last blast down the canal path out back. The bike had been pink once and had rainbow-colored clickers on the wheels that went like castanets. I knew just how the weeds poked up between the rusty spokes and how the cockeyed pedal that rubbed the chain-guard when it went around—*thunk-a-swish*—stuck up like a broken foot. The bike waved one handlebar at me.

I would've waved back, and maybe things would have been different if I had, but I was riding a motorcycle up and down the skyroad in my mind and picturing where a purse would lurch to. Then I thought maybe if we were as snowball-brained as Dawn thought, we wouldn't find it, and that would maybe mean she couldn't go anywhere right away.

From the sofa-seat of that motorcycle I could see how there was an order to things if you had a duck's worth of sense and could get it right. You started riding a bike and then you graduated to the next thing, and it was like the highway connector where one thing led to another. The road started at the truck stop—I looked back to where it began and the TRUCK STOP sign stuck up in the sky like a yellow miracle, hovering high over the rows of trucks, with their pictures of food—juicy sides of beef, bunches of frosty grapes, plates of gooey chocolate chip cookies—food bigger than our motorcycles. Everything just lined up along that road like the trucks, one after the other. The McDonald's billboard, and the ranch where we'd lived the longest of anywhere, and the Road House—even the canal lined right up.

The Road House looked like someone had dropped a big Payless shoebox into the line-up and put up a sign in front of it. No, two signs. One said ROAD HOUSE *members only* and had a picture of crossed pistons on it. The other sign rested on a bucket of sand hanging by the door and said, Put your BUTTS here.

One of the bikers, with a mohawk that made him look even taller, had a Slim Jim. I could feel the spit start under my tongue when he peeled the paper down it and bit. So I didn't mind when Cleopatra answered, yes, we could go for a ride, there was no one watching us. (Dawn was in the house, sure thing, rattling her ice in the glass and staring—but not out at us. She couldn't have known it, but our daddy had been picked up for bragging on how he'd taught the A-rab at the Pump 'n' Pantry the lesson of his life. Those foreigners thought they could come into his town and take over the place where he'd learned to pump gas when he was a kid. Dawn couldn't have been planning to take off herself, if she'd known he was in jail.)

The Harley-honker put Dooley up on the seat between his legs and asked us girls if there was any muscle on our bones, because if there was, then we could hold on on back. We two fit easy, and Cleopatra held her arms around his belt like she was shimmying up a tree, cheek to bark. I got hold of her the same way and stuck my nose into the smell of her grubby neck.

Slim Jim said, "Dell, you're not."

Our porkboy said, "Why not?"

We just zipped *BLAT* out of there, hanging on like chiggers, and that was as close to being on an airplane wing as I ever want to get.

When we got to the Silver Tooth, the porkers cut their engines and rolled around back to the basement entrance, hunkering in their seats and walking like a bunch of bugs. My skinny butt was stuck like to a La-Z-Boy, but I unpeeled. We were bowlegged as chickens, and one flap of Cleopatra's hair had jigged itself into a bass plug. We followed the smell of hot dogs. I would have gone anywhere after that smell—even the Silver Tooth.

The stools twirled in the dark. Cleopatra went into one of her staring spells the second she saw the arms on the lady bartender. It happened every time she saw a woman with fat white arms, and there was nothing for it until she decided it was or it wasn't our mother. One of the things Cleopatra could remember was our mother's round white arm going for a box of Froot Loops on the top shelf of wherever we were and knocking a mousetrap SNAP into the sink.

Dell reached back under his leather vest and pulled out, presto change-o, Dawn's purse. Slim Jim and all the rest of the pig's knuckles hooted and clapped and said how pretty. It was just macramé with a few yellow beads knotted in.

Dooley reached his spitty hand for it. Dell took the chew-toy of a wallet out and let Dooley hug the rest. Cleopatra was still eye-stuck on the bartender lady with the fat arms, so I memorized what came next. Dell opened the wallet and looked at Dawn's face under the Registry of Motor Vehicles seal. She had a ton of mascara on. He fixed on that mini-Dawn, and you could've taken bets on who'd blink first. Slim Jim muscled up behind and hoo-boyed. The rest of them were playing pool in the dark behind us. Beefaloes could have shut-up better.

Dell said, "That your mommy?"

Cleopatra said, "Not sure." She never looked anywhere but at the bartender. I said, "No, that's Dawn." Then Cleopatra swiveled on her stool and saw the purse, and you'd have thought she'd gotten a head start into the Toys for Tots collection at the Veterans Building. She held her mouth like that puppy we'd had, when he caught a grasshopper. She was maybe forgetting that if Dawn got her purse, the best girl that ever happened to us would be buying mac and cheese and Mountain Dew, putting it on the table, and going south of tomorrow before we finished chewing.

Dell said, "Does Dawn have a phone number?"

That was one sure as pie thing I knew. I knew the phone number for every place we'd ever lived. I could have told him the old motel number, or the apartment in West Virginia, or Clarendon, or Reading, or Irving, or before Dawn, in Salisbury, or the white house with the dangling shutters, I forget the town, all the way back to when my teacher taught us Your Phone Number Is The Code To Home: learn it in case you get lost. So I told him 349-, and he said, "No wait, come to the phone with me."

But the phone in the corner was miles from where the hot dogs were steaming. I said, "You get me one of them and then I will."

Slim Jim said, "You got a real horse-trader there."

Then I thought about how the money was the going-away part of the purse. So I said, "You can buy franks with the money in there," and I pointed at her little old squinchy wallet face.

He leaned his pork-belly on the bar and said, "Elsie, three dogs for our guests." Which settled it: our mother's name was Marie.

So we slathered those steamed pinkies with French's mustard and ketchup and sweet pickle relish that made my tongue smart with wanting it, and even Dooley had onions, and we heard Dell tell the phone his name was Delahunt Allen, like it was Dale Earnhardt himself, and he had found her purse and some kids with it, and would she meet him at the Silver Tooth to get them all back. While he was over there in the corner and not seeing how I was memorizing, he peeled all of the cash out of the wallet and folded it closed in his pants pocket.

So we waited for Dawn and swiveled on our stools and watched Elsie take glasses from the rack under the dusty plastic flowers and hold them crooked under the beerflow till they filled. She didn't say one thing—not even with her eyes—as she handed the beers to the hog-Harley beefomatics, who we'd known so long that soon they'd be telling us my, how we'd grown. Cleopatra shimmied up onto Dell's lap, but he said he was saving that seat, and plunked her back on her swivel stool.

When Dawn opened the door, a big slab of light tipped in. She wasn't but a mite taller than Cleopatra, and she was dressed to meet a real estate agent. She wore the white sleeveless shirt that was long enough to tuck in, the stewardess skirt, and the navy blue shoes with closed toes. The light polished her hair to a halo soft as when she'd passed out on Dooley's bed and I sneaked ahold of it so I could sleep.

I nudged Cleopatra. "Shut your yap." We'd only seen Dawn in that getup when we'd skipped out on rent and were in the market for a new place.

Dawn lifted off her sunglasses and squinted into the dark, all around from one leather-creaker to the next. Her back gave up and sagged a notch the way it does when the Chevette won't kick-to, but when she saw Dooley, who'd fallen asleep curled around the bottom of his stool, she came on in like the whole setup was nothing more than an everyday.

Dell didn't turn around, but he leaned his hammy arms on the counter and got moony-eyed at the bottles on the back wall.

Dawn said to Elsie, "You know a Delahunt Allen?"

Elsie's lips kept zipped. She wiped the counter.

Dawn said it again, but chirpy.

It took me saying, "That's him," for anything to get started.

He spun slo-mo on his stool, and I saw that he'd had his eye on Dawn all along in a mirror behind the bottles. He said, "You look different than your picture."

I could imagine her saying, "What do you expect from a mug shot, big shot?" But what she said was, "I sure appreciate you calling. Have you got my bag?" She stood with her hands in front of her, like her purse was hanging from them already, and rocked up on her bitsy shoes.

We could've eaten another hot dog in the time it took him to answer. "I have a wallet, but how do I know it's yours?"

The place got so quiet it could have been the Silver Tooth Library. She started reciting the poem of her purse. "You'll find Avon lipstick named 'Moonbeam Misbegotten.' A half a pack of Marlboros. Two gold hoop earrings."

"No. No. No. I'm talking wallet," he said all teacher-y. "What's in your wallet?"

She sighed. "My license, which you saw. And my money."

"How much money?"

She made a face like she'd just eaten a clam and had to spit. "There's a hundred and seventy-three bucks."

Cleopatra said, "You got that much money?"

Dawn said, "Shut."

Dell flapped open her wallet in his palm like he was about to butter it. "This one must not be yours, cuz there's nothing more than about a hundred seventy three cents."

If I'd been sitting where Cleopatra was, I'd have grabbed it faster than a pickpocket. I'd have been slap gone, faster than a no-see-um, into the ditch by the street, where, if I had to, I would have waited until the beefalo army'd gone to church.

Dawn just put her sunglasses back on and said, "If that's all you're giving back, I'll need a drink." She asked Elsie, "A hundred seventy-three cents enough for a shot of bourbon?"

Elsie poured a glass and left it.

Dell said, "That's all that was in it." He clapped the wallet shut. "Except for the three bucks that bought these kids lunch." With his paw, he trapped it on the bar. "What are you offering for a reward?"

I was sure that now Dawn's tongue would pull free of the flypaper. She was looking all around. But she just whispered, "I thanked you."

He said out loud, "I didn't have to call you." He said, "I think maybe, say, a ten dollar reward. That would do it."

Dawn flipped her empty hands, palms and backs, like a nothing-up-my-sleeve magician. Her arms were smooth and pink like a doll's. "Oh, I'll just reach right into the spare money clip I carry at all times," she said, "and hand you what you want, Delahunt Allen." She turned to Dooley, sleeping with the rest of her purse on the floor, "Dooley-boy, hand your Mommy that ten-spot we keep in your ear." His eyelids didn't even flicker. "Oh, don't have it this time? What about you Cleopatra? Can't keep track of a dime? Don't worry, honey, Kaylene's going to run a bank when she grows up. She thinks she's real smart that way." She barely looked at me. "Right, Kaylene? Why don't you give the man what he's asking for?"

So while Dawn ran her mouth, I hopped off my stool. I didn't like his leather smell, but that wasn't going to stop me doing what she asked. When I pushed my fingers into his pants pocket, he backhanded me, and I hit the bar and went down like a rag doll between the stools.

So, maybe I'm not the best one to tell the rest of this story. I'd guess Dawn tried to do something about me laying like a piece of meat at her feet. I don't think she would have cried—I wasn't Dooley. I can picture her squatting by me in her hoity-toity skirt and pumps, wagging my chops from side to side, and then trying to make me hold ice on my face, but I didn't wake up until later. She might have let fly a few opinions about calling the cops, but Dell would have just bought her another drink.

Maybe this story's just like all of them. A road-hog with a hard-on buys a little blonde one double bourbon after another, using her very own cash to do it, until she's dancing on the bar and laughing into his tattoo, and then all the pig-warriors rumble off with their pretty door prize, and we discover there's more than one way to make Cleopatra cry.

Later that night, Cleopatra sniffled while we twirled on our stools in the empty bar. I never did get any ice on my face. Elsie made one phone call after another. She couldn't stop talking then, saying into the phone, what is she supposed to do with three kids, her job is to close the bar—that's her job—three kids that aren't hers, in the middle of the night. She and her fat arms. She kept switching the lights off one by one by one while she talked. And we kept hoping that since we had darling Dooley with us, Dawn would make the hog-washers bring her back.

I blame my jack-lick brain for not seeing where Elsie's phone calls were pointing us. Sometimes I think, if only I'd been behind Cleopatra, maybe I would have seen her put the purse on the Chevette. Or maybe if I'd been sharper, I could have noticed it, maybe heard it, sliding across the roof and saucering off the back. Then everything in this story could have lined up some other way: it would go back and back, to where it could straighten out. Maybe it would be like a river, the Merrimack, winding around to where Dawn would have had her purse and could have bought our supper at Clint's Mart, and what happened from there would stretch out differently, get right, as we rolled forward. But what can you expect? Pigeon crap's got more smarts than me.

I still don't know if Dawn knew where our daddy'd got to. I've got to believe she didn't, and maybe she still doesn't. The next day, the people at County Social Services toddled Dooley down the office hallway and shut the door, and that was the last we ever saw of him, or Dawn, either.

Anyone with more than shit for dirt between her ears could have told you that we wouldn't be going back to that house by the highway connector. I missed all the signs. I hadn't even seen that my rusty bicycle—waving over the weeds—was saying good-bye to me.

Frankie Floats

FRANKIE BURROUGHS HAD WALKED OFF THE FOUR-STORY ROOF OF THE OLD Hub Hosiery building that had once belonged to his grandfather. Now he was trying to buy cigarettes. The sign off the Lowell Connector said, "Pump 'n' Pantry," and promised "gro bev cigs gas," but no one was behind the counter.

Trying not to slur his words, he said, "Anyone home?" But he was still fucked up. A radio on the top shelf whined out a tune, something Middle Eastern that twisted in his gut. Why did these chrome and glass places with the gas pumps out front have to be lit like operating rooms? "Where is everyone?" Over by the doughnuts, the coffee machines were all on, burning the stuff to sludge.

A surveillance screen above the register, clicking from vacant aisle to aisle, showing the shelves at weird angles in black and white, gave him vertigo. The smell of burnt coffee didn't help. He planted his feet on the floor, carefully, as if he were placing a ladder, and leaned on the counter. The screen displayed him in all his youth, his big square head, and the stocky body he couldn't trust. Maybe cigarettes did stunt your growth. Look at him: Frankie, the walking miracle, shorter than anyone in his fucked-up family—the people who insisted on calling him Franklin, as if he could be presidential.

There'd been a miracle, but he wasn't it. The vinyl roof of a black Cadillac parked on the street below had broken his fall. He wanted to tell someone. He'd thought of calling his kid sister. Hey, Helen, did you know drunks bounce? But he hadn't spoken to her for months.

He'd done a number on the car—dented the roof so it looked like an old mattress. He didn't remember taking that wrong step. He'd always thought a long fall would feel like flying. It was more like floating, followed by a dive. He must have hung for a second like Wile E. Coyote before plunging.

He knocked on the plastic sign hanging above him, LOTTERY TICKETS SOLD HERE. "Hey, heads up!" he said. "You got Wile E. Coyote, the dog himself, paying a visit." He kept talking even with his words shimmying up against each other. "Yeah, the dog himself, standing here in your fucking convenience store, and he's wondering where the exact fuck convenience comes into it." He suppressed his nausea and waved a ten-dollar bill at the camera. "He wants a smoke. He really wants a smoke." Where'd he found ten bucks? For the benefit of the camera, he pointed at the signs—"Newport," "Kool,"—and put two fingers in a V by his rounded mouth. The Marlboros he wanted lay just a reach away.

Was it his fault there'd been no railing on the roof? Who has a party on a roof with no railing? He twisted around looking for someone, anyone. "Hey, I could be dead. But I'm here. See that good-looking guy on the TV screen?" He flipped his hair out of his face. "I'm scaring myself with could-be-dead, why isn't anyone here?"

He turned and slouched down the first aisle, swerving safely past the

Pringles and the Cheetos, thinking, *See me? I'm passing up all this would-be food and reaching for a box of Triscuits, a box of all-American whole-grain goodness. If I open this box and eat it, will you come?* He couldn't eat, though; the nausea crept in, so he felt like he was falling again. If you hit a car instead of the other way around, and you run away, is that a hit and run? He put the Triscuits back and said, out loud: "I walked away." It began to scare him, but then he remembered Patricia. The girl who had driven him. Waiting outside. She must have been the one who said, "Drunks bounce, don't you know?" She'd held a cigarette like she was going to bite it and said, "You don't know much, do you?" She wouldn't lend him a smoke. "Quit whining, and get your own." She'd pulled in under the Pump 'n' Pantry sign, and said, "What a pain in the ass."

He stuck his head out the door. The door hit the bells hanging from the ceiling. He swung it open and shut, ringing the bells, hitting them back and forth. He couldn't see where Patricia had parked. Was that even her name? Around the pumps, the lot was lit as brightly as the store. Beyond, black night.

Quickly, he stepped back behind the counter, lifted a carton of Marlboros, and keeping his balance, headed for the parking lot.

It was empty. Straight white parking lines shone brightly. Asphalt curbs so fresh they smelled of tar, and flowers, marigolds, planted around the lampposts in perfect circles. Fuck. What had she been driving? He remembered a red interior, air freshener hanging from the mirror. A rusty little shit box. A Toyota? Whatever. She'd gone. Just what friends are for. She'd left him with nothing but the rank smell of gasoline and highway ramps circling away into the dark.

He had no place to go and no way to get there. Who planted flowers at a gas station? He eased himself back inside without sounding the bells. He might be able to keep down a Coke. A little tobacco, a little Coke, he'd find his cool.

When he opened the fridge door, he heard a man's voice and spun toward the counter. But it was only the radio giving the news in Arabic or whatever they spoke wherever the hell convenience store owners came from. Persia. People from that part of the world said they were from Persia like that was so different from Iran. He said, "I'm from PERsia," and twisted the top off his drink. He couldn't remember when he'd eaten.

His kid sister, the food queen, would tell him he needed protein: "Dig into the cheese, Franklin."

He asked his Coke, "What are you now, my nutritionist?"

He would have told Helen falling off the roof had been like floating. Gravity had no power. And then suddenly every blood vessel in him felt the pull, and he knew what it was like to be the cat he used to get stoned. What was its name? Her cat. Peanutbutter. He and Peanutbutter would get wasted up on the roof of their house on Fairmont Avenue. That cat loved pot. Frankie would climb the fire escape, and she'd follow him by scooting up the nearest beech tree. She'd sit in front of him squinting while he blew smoke at her. She'd knead the pebbles on the flat part of the roof and purr. What a twisted little animal. Frankie hunkered against the warm slate of a dormer while Peanutbutter rubbed against everything on that roof, the chimney, his shins, the toilet vents, the fire escape, his boots, until she got to the gutter. That was the best. She thrust her chin, her cheeks, and her neck along that satisfying edge. He'd watch as she rubbed herself right off. It was a long way down, but she always landed on her feet.

He guzzled the rest of his Coke, sat on the floor at the back of the store, and opened the Marlboros. Shelter from the storm. He leaned against the flimsy shelving—Progresso Kidney Beans, Franco-American Spaghetti and Meatballs. He'd discovered the surveillance camera's blind spot. He'd always known how to hide. It was his specialty, disappearing. Couldn't remember where he lived some days, but he never forgot this: everyone's got a blind spot.

His shoulder was sore. Was that all? You fall four flights and your shoulder has complaints? From behind the radio announcer's voice came a whimpering noise, as if he held someone hostage in his radio booth. Frankie didn't know which was worse, news delivered in a foreign language or foreign music. He lit his cigarette. The rush, like a song flowing through him, reached to the tips of his fingers. He felt himself smoothing out.

He stretched out on the floor. From that angle, the store was a crammed kaleidoscope of red and yellow and black. Cans, boxes, bags. Great New Taste! All New Recipe! Original Flavor! Wise. Mr. Peanut. Salted. Unsalted. Wow, new flavor burst! The only quiet spot in his view was a fire extinguisher on the bare wall above the ice cream cooler. Patti? Tricia? He pictured her running toward the store. She could be shouting, "My car is on fire!" He tried to make it sexy. Her boobs bouncing as she ran, terror stretching her boring face into something hot and needy, a ring glinting in her navel, but the truth was, her sneakers would *splat splat* on the new asphalt, and her rubbery hips would bulge over the top of her jeans. She'd jostle across the parking lot. But before she even got to the door, he'd be running with the fire extinguisher. He'd grab it off the wall without thinking, just a speedy reflexive action perfectly tuned to the situation. No fuss, no mess, he'd take care of it. He wouldn't think of himself as a hero, just a guy doing what was needed. He'd shoot foam all around the undercarriage of that crappy car. She'd be so grateful, she'd give him a ride home. Or no, that wouldn't work. She'd phone a friend who'd drive them home. Except he had nowhere to go.

He'd had a setup behind the boiler in the Hub Mills condo building he'd walked off—bedding that folded into an innocuous-looking box, all the *National Geographic*s a guy could ever want piled against the cellar wall. For lousy weather, he had his old sheepskin coat stuffed under the window frame—nothing but a bit of insulation to the unsuspecting eye. A rusty toilet and sink by the bulkhead stairs took care of him. But he couldn't go back to that basement, even though the building had once been his ancestors' sweatshop. The Cadillac that saved him was always parked out front. Frankie had left it looking like it had flipped in a rollover, the windshield shattered, the roof caved. The car could belong to the building's super for all he knew. He remembered the faces peering down at him over the edge of the roof.

The radio launched into more whiney music. He could turn it off, but that would mean getting up. He could take a nap—he could swivel the OPEN sign, lock the door, and settle in. He had provisions to last a lifetime.

He'd simply followed the sound of a party up the stairs to where the bounty awaited him, fine food and drink spread from one side of the roof deck to the other. The wind blew, and it was a party on top of the old hosiery mill that had made his family wealthy, and spring had come to the city, and he wasn't going to question his good fortune in finding his way there. The Ouellette Bridge was all lit up, and the tops of the old smoke stacks, down what people still called the mile of mills, flashed red. Very festive. The dark had settled, so maybe they wouldn't notice how he wasn't exactly dressed for it, or that he was a shade young. A lady in a suit eyed him like she knew he didn't belong. Frankie could bet he'd parked her Mercedes a few times when he had that gig at the garage, so he just put a little crowd between them and kept helping himself. A cornucopia of delights, and didn't they know their single-malt scotches?

When he heard a sound like a car door shutting, he thought how it would be if someone else came into the store. This place felt like his for the night. He could scream if he wanted to. He hadn't screamed when he fell, and now the memory of falling just made him quiet. He wanted to be quiet. He peeked over a hand-painted sign in the window that said SODA, ICE CREAM, CANDY. No one and nothing moved in the lot. He fiddled with the deadbolt on the door until it slipped into place. He flipped the CLOSED sign.

Once when he was a kid, he'd gotten left in a clothing store on Market Street while the woman behind the counter and his mother, Delia, locked the door behind them and hurried to get a drink across the street. He'd tried the knob. He'd knocked his hands on the glass. The women crossed the street, their lipstick very red, their mouths moving fast. He'd thought his mother would look down and not see him and come rushing back. But she barely took her eyes off the other lady's face.

He had run his hand along the soft skirts hanging on a circular rack—the smell like the blanket box at home. He pushed his head into them, eyes shut. It was quiet, the air still as a closet. He felt very safe, as if he'd been tucked into bed in a dark room. He climbed into the center of the skirt rack and fell asleep. A scout in his tent.

Now Frankie's bladder tugged on him, urging him to find the toilet. What a boy scout. Bladder the size of a walnut.

Passing the checkout counter, he stepped on and broke something like a miniature plastic spear. A flagpole without a flag, from the box of American flags standing at attention by the cash register in rows as straight as a cemetery. He picked the stripped flagpole off the floor—making the room spin—and tossed the pieces onto the counter.

The key was in the cash register. Waving like a little hand.

The surveillance camera shifted on its arm by the door. He watched it, timing its moves, but by now, it would have nabbed him front, back, and side, the complete portrait. It knew the exact gray of the sweatshirt he wore, the tired pants, even the make of his high-tops. Whatever the register held had to stay there.

He fished five bucks from one of his pockets and thirty from the other. The wadded five, a stray from the sale of his father's camera. He knew all about that, but the rest? He stared at the twenty, at Andrew Jackson's folded face, which was as long as his mother's. Frankie said, "Look at me, fucker." Jackson's eyes pointed nowhere but into the past. Those lips were sealed. He'd give no clues to how he'd gotten in Frankie's pocket. Two steps away there might be a drawerful just like him.

Frankie eased in behind the counter, where the outlook was new and different. Jars of little aspirin packs and Slim Jims lined the shelf. Batteries and shoelaces, duct tape, key chains, and a giant plastic model of a Cool Dog—ice cream in a cakey bun with chocolate "ketchup" and whipped cream "mustard." When he was a kid, he'd devoured one of those every time he got to Fenway Park, but now the sight of it turned his stomach.

He dragged the stool up to the register. Something thumped. What had he bumped? He could lounge here, nod to his customers and say, "How're you doing?" like a host, like his father offering cocktails to his guests—olive or a twist? Press the keys and ask, "Did you find everything you need today?" Punch the keys, hammer the long one with the heel of his hand like an old pro. *Ching.* But he didn't.

His mother had come back to the clothing store for him, in the end.

She'd crawled into the skirt rack laughing, "He's in here. The little minx-ie's hiding." The smell of what she'd been drinking had filled the space where he slept.

He'd maybe take a peek in the cash register, but first, he needed the bathroom. A restroom sign pointed the way between counter and coffee machines. Boxes of Cottonelle bathroom tissue leaned against the wall, narrowing the hallway. He unzipped as he shoved open the bathroom door, except the door didn't give.

His shoulder did. Pain filtered through—a couple feet either way and they'd have had to scrape him off the street. He had walked away. Now a shiver began in one leg, surging through him until the loneliness of his luck rattled in his bones—deep—where he carried everything, nowhere he could reach. He had rolled off the smashed car roof, and the girl, Patricia, had stopped for him. She'd seen it happen and treated him like some kind of superhero until she'd gotten to know him. Now his shoulder and his shaking legs and his bursting bladder told him just how alive he was. Using his other shoulder, he pushed on the restroom door again. It wasn't locked. Something heavy blocked it.

He leaned on the door and pushed his eye to the crack. He scanned, narrowly: a slice of wall, a cheap ceiling fixture, a sink, the toilet handle, the pipes under the sink, and a small American flag taped over the nose and mouth of a man on the floor. Soft brown ear, broken and bloody. Black hair. Frankie jumped back and landed loudly on the Cottonelle boxes.

He rubbed his knees wildly, trying to stop the shaking. Had he seen right? He eased his eye back to the crack.

Was anything moving? The man's eyes were closed. Thick eyelashes. Could he breathe? Frankie tried to push the door wider, but he was afraid he'd hurt the man worse.

Almost within Frankie's reach, an old pay phone hung on the wall. He could feel the weight of the phone receiver as if he'd lifted it already. Didn't he know what it was to get up and walk away? He'd keep cool while the phone rang wherever emergency calls ring. The ambulance would come, efficient EMTs with a gurney and belts with clasps like seat belts to click tight. He could see—dizzyingly—the revolving light from the ambulance, blue then red, the aisles of junk food pulsing.

He would say—what would he say? How would he explain? He'd only wanted cigarettes. He'd done his best. He'd tried to pay for them. He *could* pay for them. And the surveillance tape, the locked door?

What if the guy wasn't breathing? A plaid shirt. Frankie tried to hold steady long enough to see him move. The man's eyelid released, popped half-open, swollen rimmed, blood-shot. Moist. The shock of that slight motion detonated in Frankie, sent him scrambling, knocking the pay phone receiver off its hook. He spun with the pain, clamping his shoulder. He felt as exposed as if caught by a camera's flash, the loser revealed. His time here was up. He had to go, but the phone dangled, humming—insisting he pay attention to what mattered. That guy could be alive.

Frankie grabbed the phone. The cold silver buttons gave as he pushed them. 911. A low beep and two high ones in his ear.

"What is your emergency?" A woman's voice.

It wasn't his, the emergency. Whatever had happened here was not anything to do with him. That man could maybe be alive, but either way he was not Frankie's business. Frankie didn't know anything about him. He had never seen him before. No. This was not his problem.

"Hello, your emergency? I see you're at 1407 Lowell Connector. Is that correct?"

Frankie's eyes were doing something weird. Even when he shut them tight and held his breath, he felt his vision opening out as if he were rising—he couldn't stop it. His view widened even with his eyes squeezed closed. He floated higher, higher than a high wire act, until he looked down on the Mobil station—nothing to save him. Nothing to say it wasn't Frankie who did that to the man.

"Hello? Can you confirm?"

He kept his eyes jammed shut and held his breath. He saw the little man way down below, and the aisles of food and cigarettes, and the tiny gas pumps under circles of light, and the litter of his own life strewn wide over the parking lot, like wreckage from a plane. If he didn't do something different, he would have to let whatever this meant into his head. It would be another thing he would have to remember. One more wrong step.

Frankie needed air. He breathed desperately in and out until the steady hum of being alive flowed into him. He opened his eyes. Just this side of gone, he stood, his feet on the floor. He held the receiver to his ear and exhaled his answer to the woman, "Yes."

He dropped the phone and backed down the narrow hall away from the voice asking for more. He pushed off from this mistake that wasn't his in the Pump 'n' Pantry restroom—moving now, breathing—fumbling the deadbolt open, feeling the ground beneath his sneakers, jolts of pain in his shoulder—through the newly painted parking lot, and over the curb that reeked of tar. He ran under the on-ramp and away, to someplace he could let it all go, somewhere no one could find him.

Copper Leaves Waving

AFTER FRANKLIN LEFT, DR. AND MRS. BURROUGHS WAITED FOR THE PHONE to ring. Evening after evening, they waited, nursing martinis and dwindling like stick dolls. When their refrigerator was emptied of all but a jar of cocktail olives and some old butter, Helen, their daughter, moved up to the maid's quarters in their house on Belvidere Hill and stuffed the little kitchen there with groceries delivered from Lowell Provisions, where they had a charge account.

Helen was seventeen and danced in front of the mirror for hours. The ancient beech trees pressed in toward the windows as if her third-floor apartment were a tree house. The branches swayed, the copper leaves shimmied, and she watched her tall, slim body dip and turn far above the street. She danced to anything with a strong beat. She swung her long hair.

To get boys upstairs was relatively easy. Since her brother, Franklin, took off, she'd fallen in love every time a boy came knocking. She'd hear the *twang* and *thonk* of feet on the fire escape and then the solid promise of knuckles on the old glass of the window. They came up the fire escape, because if they took the inside route they had to get around her brother's dog. The Burroughs never understood what Franklin wanted, but they'd guessed he ought to be made responsible for something that would love him. The dog looked like Lassie but in an irritatingly small size, and its love lasted far beyond Franklin's being responsible. The dog would go off like firecrackers when anyone but Franklin came into the house.

The boys found Helen at school or walking home or hanging around in Kerouac Square. They liked to see themselves reflected in her big brown eyes. They wanted to know, was she a model, or would she model? Could they take her picture, could they carry her books, take her to dinner, take her to bed? They liked her skin, which was very smooth. They liked her pouty lower lip. They loved her.

And afterward, she would stir up some spices and sour cream in a bright red bowl. It was a little ritual. She'd sit with the comforter pulled up to her waist, the shadows of the trees moving over her bed, and she'd trail sweet yellow peppers in figure eights through the creamy dip until they were gone. The boys saw themselves out.

Ken Chang lasted longer than the others. No one in their neighborhood had the poor taste to question an Asian boy climbing a fire escape, maybe because he wore glasses and carried a viola case. He knocked on her window. Ken Chang's body was almost hairless and made her feel like a waterfall.

After a while, it wasn't satisfying just to get him upstairs without anyone noticing, so once when no one was home, she led Ken down to her parents' bed in the heart of the house. He lifted her blouse off. His clean fingers, with their trimmed cuticles and tiny calluses, strummed each of her ribs. She imagined his fingers pressing on the strings of his viola, pressing, pressing, and she had to lie down.

Somewhere in the middle of things, she said, "Stop. Just stop."

Ken went still; he was a mild boy. The view from her parents' bed had emptied her. Through the window, she'd seen the outlines of her father's garden, which had once spanned the property. Boxwoods choked the paths, and the only thing still growing was parsley, a tangled patch. Beyond the garden, beautiful old houses with their stately trees lined Fairmont Avenue, where she and Franklin and the other neighborhood kids used to play cops and robbers, or sardines—until Franklin got so good at hiding that no one would play with him. He had perfected finding the space where no one would think to look—always a new place—and he would fold himself into it, something like the opposite of Houdini, leaving the other children wandering in packs, aimless and dissatisfied, wanting to give up. He had a talent.

Did her parents lie in this bed waiting as silently as they sat in the music room? Did they lie here not talking, not touching, two tall, thin, gray people making no more noise than the smoke that wafted up from their cigarettes?

Helen put her hands over her eyes to shut out the hollowness.

Then she heard the back door clunk open, and far away, the down stairs floorboards creaked. She hadn't thought about what her parents were going to do if they caught her. What could they do? That was the thing about them: what could they do?

She and Ken moved fast, pulling on their clothes as they went, but they weren't thinking and moved in the wrong direction, into the dead end of the dressing room with its amber light, where they exchanged a trapped look and Ken pushed her mother's hairbrush into her hand, whispering, "You're completely disheveled."

It was Franklin who stuck his big head around the corner. His face was drawn, pale, and unshaven. His hair, which was so much lighter than anyone else's in the family, had been hacked off unevenly. He was shorter and older than she remembered. He didn't look well nourished. With his head going side to side, as if he had a current running through him, he looked at her with her blouse inside out, hairbrush in hand, and then at Ken who seemed peculiarly naked, fleshy, without his glasses. Her face and throat went hot. Franklin's eyes were so neutral, so empty of surprise or pleasure or even recognition that she wanted to bite him or beat him, to go at him, flailing. Ken put his arm out, stopping her.

Franklin laughed in a way that sounded like it hurt. He laughed as he used to when he'd twist her arm up behind her back—a tight sound that seemed to cost him. His grubby gray sweatshirt shook. His eyes didn't change, vacant and blue. As if after months of her not knowing where he was, it made no difference that he was standing right there, within reach of her fury, or her love.

He said, "I should've known. In their bed. Don't let me interrupt." She couldn't breathe. His legs and arms looked wired onto him, like a puppet's. He couldn't hold still, but flipped his sweatshirt hood up and spun from them, past her mother's dressing table with its array of perfume bottles and sprays, saying, "I'm gone." It seemed he was turning forever, in that brownish light, spinning away from her, his limbs all loose and jangly, and she would never be able to breathe again.

He had swung around into the hallway and taken the stairs down, two, three at a time, before she yelled, "How dare you? Where are you going?" He had shut the door after him by the time she said, "Wait. No. Don't go."

Later, when their parents found he'd taken all of their liquor—every bottle gone—Helen went into Franklin's room, as if being there would help her know what was happening. There was nothing on the walls but three rolled bits of masking tape left from a dead rock star's poster. His room smelled like a storage closet. Underneath, though, was the odor of something like old socks and yard dirt. She sat on his bed.

For a while after he had discovered his gift for disappearing, he had let her hide with him while he practiced on their unsuspecting father. Franklin led her up the built-in shelves in the pantry to the top of the liquor closet. When they sat up, he could almost touch the high ceiling. He showed her how to lie in the dust with her hands tight at her sides. They pulled their shoulders up toward their ears to fit the narrow space. A raised molding kept them from rolling off.

Franklin smelled sharply of grass stains and boy sweat. The expression he wore when he was hiding, or thinking about hiding, was the same expression he'd had when he'd told her he couldn't say why he had to carry a picture of Tonto folded in his shoe like a dollar bill, he just had to, until softball season was over. He was fairer and much stronger than she would ever be. His brow knit like an older person's when he shushed her—intent on disappearance, on doing it right. She couldn't help admiring him.

Night after night, they climbed up there, he adding up the times until they were discovered and he would have to find a new spot; she, so hungry for dinner there was nothing else to do but wait for their father to come home from work and get the cocktails made. She'd study the ceiling cracks to keep from wriggling, to keep as still as Franklin.

He'd pinch her skinny hip. "Get your legs flat," and show her, with his knobby kid knees locked in position, how to be invisible. He wanted their father to stand right below them unknowing, to come that close, reaching for the martini glasses—his hand just inches below them—without ever knowing they were there. Helen longed for a sneaker lace to be hanging down, or for one of them to breathe too loudly. She hoped that as their father filled the ice bucket, or fixed the tray, one of their stomachs would growl and startle him, or else that their mother would remember they were there and give him some sort of signal—anything so they would be noticed and could rise up on their elbows and present him with the fact of themselves. She wanted nothing more than for her father to look up and see them before he took the cocktails into the music room, even if he only said, "Haven't you got anything better to do than give an old man a coronary?"

The house felt as if Franklin could still be there somewhere, squeezed into the closet with the hot water heater, or folded onto a shelf with the linens. She wished she could see that old mixture of defeat and pride in his eyes when he was discovered.

She sat on Franklin's bed and wiped the dust off his wooden music box with the flat of her hand. It had an uneven red stripe. The varnish had cracked. When they were younger, he would never let anyone touch it. When he was in the bathroom or the hall, she used to run into his room and flip the lid open just to bug him. Her mother had given it to him when he was little, before Helen was born. Helen didn't want to hear its sad little plinking song now. His boombox had been forgotten under the desk. She didn't feel like listening to that either. Their parents had given it to him so he would have something to do while he was shut away in his room. Which, before he left, was all the time. That became his way of being there without being there. She couldn't imagine what he did but sit behind the door that shut them out, flipping his hair out of his face. At least then she'd known where he was.

Sitting there on the bed that had been made up as if he'd be home any minute, she understood that he wouldn't be. In her mind, she saw him again as he'd been in the amber light of the dressing room with Ken. She saw him spinning away, and away from her with his hood up, turning and raveling the air.

↜

Franklin returned regularly, when their parents weren't home, but at first, it was only to clean out the liquor cabinet. He didn't look for her or let her know when he was there. She could tell he'd been back whenever she heard her father's Rover pull in from work, heard the dog yap its head off in the hallway as usual, and then heard the car, almost immediately, pull out again. She'd hear her mother fill the ice bucket and cross the bare hallway in her pumps, the same as any night. The only difference was, the silence that followed came from her mother waiting alone.

From the shadows of the front stairwell, Helen could see her mother sitting in the corner of the music room, wearing her usual sweater and tweed skirt. The way she crossed her legs in the wing chair still gave an impression of old money and grace, as if she'd been somebody once. She'd have two glasses on the table. An olive in one. A twist of lemon in the other. Except to light a cigarette, she wouldn't move until Helen's father returned from Clint's Mart with the new bottles. A white princess phone sat quiet as a bouquet in the center of the cocktail table.

For a while, the only word from Franklin was his emptying clean the liquor supply. But around the time that Helen moved on from Ken Chang, Franklin's boombox vanished. Next, it was the video equipment they'd gotten him when they thought he might get interested in something. Then he took the pillow from his bed, and she thought maybe he had an apartment. But another time, he took his sheepskin coat, and she just knew he was living on the street. She didn't know what he would do next.

He started in on their parents' belongings, and she guessed he was selling them. He didn't try to hide the fact that things were disappearing. The TV, he just lifted away, leaving its shape in the dust on the table, its outlet exposed. Where the stereo speakers had been in the bookshelf, he left gaps, like missing teeth. Where sunlight was supposed to fall just *so* on one of Degas's dancers, the sculpture's pedestal stood vacant.

One evening, her father stopped Helen on her way upstairs. He kept his gray hair cut close and wore a jacket and tie. People mistook him for the faded-handsome Nobel-winning economist from up the street, but he was a doctor in the infirmary of a boys' school. His hand seemed always to be smoothing the hair on the back of his head or patting his jacket, his pockets, vaguely. He looked through the balusters and asked, "Helen, do you know the whereabouts of your mother's topaz ring?"

She hadn't heard that many words out of her father's mouth for weeks. She snapped, "Are you accusing me now?"

"We just wanted to check that you didn't know anything about it."

"You'd think he could go for something more creative."

Her mother's voice wafted out into the hall. "That topaz never fit the setting very well." Helen and her father turned toward her voice. "I didn't wear it much anyway."

Helen asked, "Didn't that ring belong to your grandmother?"

Her mother didn't answer her.

"Wasn't it, someday, going to be mine?" Helen squinted at her father who was still turned toward her mother. "Are you just going to let him take it, take everything, piece by piece?"

He said, "She's right, Delia. This has got to stop." To no one in particular he said, "There's got to be an end to this."

The Burroughs invited the police to come over, as if it were a social call. They didn't want Helen in the room, but she overheard one of the cops say, "If he's going to behave like a criminal, you've got to treat him like one."

So, they changed the locks and put one on the liquor cabinet. Helen had a buzzer installed for her apartment. She just didn't want to have to go all the way downstairs to let in her new boyfriend, Chester.

Chester Harrison said a college man shouldn't be climbing fire escapes. Being resourceful enough to carry dog biscuits, he would come in the back door. He reminded her of a pretty tin soldier, compact with a tightly trimmed mustache, pink cheeks, and tasseled loafers. He was a little shorter than she, which she didn't especially like. Chester taught her that a copper bowl and a wire whisk are required to make a proper omelet.

Two or three times, the buzzer rang when she didn't expect him, and when she buzzed him in, he didn't come up. It seemed an inexplicable thing, like smoke detectors going off when it was humid. But one evening, after the bell rang and no one showed up, her mother came upstairs and knocked on the door. She appeared so distant and burdened she might as well have been the Queen.

"To what do I owe this honor?" Helen asked. Standing on the top step, her mother looked as old as the Marabou bird in *Babar*. Since Franklin started stealing, she'd gone beyond gray. The circles under her eyes were stains, and Helen imagined that instead of blood, tobacco smoke and booze ran through her mother's veins.

Her mother asked, "Have you been letting Franklin in?"

Helen said, "No," but as she said it, she realized she had been. "Maybe I did without knowing it."

"Your grandmother's silverware is gone. It was all I had of my mother."

She paused, but what could Helen say?

She continued, "We've spoken to the detective, and he has advised us: if your doorbell rings, see who it is. Look out your window, and if it's Franklin, call the police. You're supposed to say, 'There's someone ringing my doorbell and he won't go away.'" She reached a shaky hand to tuck away a loose strand of her hair. "Can you say that?"

Helen recited, "There is someone ringing my doorbell and he will not go away."

"Helen. It has been very difficult getting to this point." Then she looked past her daughter into the hallway and asked, "Do you have everything you need?"

A few days later, while Helen danced, barefoot on the Oriental rug, watching her hips sway in the mirror, the copper leaves waving in the windows behind her, the bell rang. Helen turned off the music and, instead of pressing the buzzer, went to look out her bedroom window. Through the bars of the fire escape, she saw Franklin pacing the back stoop like a chained dog. He wore black high-tops and clothes she'd never seen before. He could have been anyone. He leaned on the bell again. She didn't buzz him in. He pointed his finger and pressed so the bell in the hallway screamed impatiently.

The old black phone waited on the table. The receiver was heavy in her hand, smooth and cold. Helen dialed nine and one and one, hearing each of the clicks sounding down the wire, out of the house and far away, as the dial rotated back into place. She said the words she was supposed to say and floated back to the front room. She didn't dance. The doorbell rang again and again. Through the beech boughs, she saw three police cars swerve off Fairmont Avenue into the drive. No sirens. They came so fast she thought they were going to crash. She ran back to her bedroom to see if her brother was still on the porch.

Franklin cannonballed into her room from the fire escape. The window sash splintered like kindling. Glass exploded. He rolled, ending up on the floor at her feet. In the gaping quiet that followed, he lay there, a full-grown man curled with his arms around his head, breathing on her floor. Bits of glass glittered all over him in the dappled light that fell through the beech trees.

He'd made a hole in the house. Air rushed in, and she balanced, feeling nothing between her and the trees—feeling the void on every side of her. Hollow, lonely air.

Then she kicked him. She kicked him hard in the kidney, hard enough to hurt her foot.

Her foot connected with his back, and the solidity of him hammered back and blossomed through her. This was her brother. The shock of it flowed up her leg and through her belly and her arms and her neck. She'd called the police. She teetered there in the tower of her room, the window blown out, black splinters of sash on the red rug, glass everywhere. The shock of what she'd done filled her to brimming.

He uncurled and gathered himself up—to protect himself, she thought—but he held his palms up somewhere between surprise and a shrug and whispered, "I'm sorry. Sorry. Sorry."

They heard feet on the fire escape. He looked wildly at her, and before she could do anything more—he took off down through the house. She heard the front door slam.

The police combed the neighborhood. Franklin's dog paced. Helen was convinced Franklin was still in the house. She might have been confusing the feeling of having found him—of having made hard contact for that instant—with a feeling of nearness. She looked everywhere. She looked where no one but Franklin would think to hide. It would be a new place, but just in case, she looked in places he'd hidden before, too. Exultation, or something like it, filled her for those hours. Was it hope? Something new would begin now.

She thought to look on top of the liquor cabinet. He had grown much too big for it, but she pulled a chair to the front. As she stepped up, she had a view through the window to the front yard. In the shadowy hollow in the base of the oldest beech tree, she caught sight of his feet, his black high-tops. He was inside the tree.

By then, the tree was what held him upright. He'd used a syringe to send a bubble to his heart.

There was not one particular moment that haunted her, not the phoning, or when she kicked him, or when she found him, or after, when she had to tell what had happened. She could be on her way to work, years later, after she had left Lowell and moved to Boston. She would look up from the detective story she was reading, and instead of the usual diagram of routes posted on the subway wall, she'd see their old house on once tony Fairmont Avenue. In place of the intersecting metro lines of red and green—with the Alewife stop at the bottom, and the blue line going off at an angle past State Street at the top—she saw the amber of her mother's dressing room, the green of her father's parsley persisting in the garden, her red bedroom rug. She looked away. But the house, like a map of her growing up, went wherever she looked. YOU ARE HERE.

There was nothing to mediate her vision of alcoves and closets, the quiet rooms, the cubby under the stairs. Dappled shadows falling across her bed. The chipped black enamel of the fire escape.

She wouldn't see her own reflection in the dark glass of the train window, staring back with eyes not unlike her mother's. She wouldn't be aware of the passengers around her leaning as the train took a turn, or how, next to her, the man in a suit was willing her to notice him. All she could see were the big gray rooms where the ceilings were so high it felt like a layer was missing, where smoke from a cigarette uncoiled, drifted up, and hung.

Cantogallo

For Nadia Diego
Deported September 2005

FROM OUTSIDE IZABEL'S DREAM, A MAN'S VOICE SAID, "HEY!" HE SHOVED HIS face close to hers. "Do you hear me?"

Izabel rarely held still, but she'd come to a stop on the stoop. She slept—a slippery little muscle of a girl—with her arm folded under her cheek on the top step. She had been dreaming that her sister Lina was home safe from Iraq because of something to do with Izabel's special red sneakers.

The man smelled of cigarettes. "Is your mother home?" he said.

Her mother was hardly ever home. She cleaned houses with Rupert Araújo's mother, who lived upstairs. Rupert and Izabel were home alone.

"Maybe it's *your* rooster that thinks day begins at three in the morning," he said. He was the man from across the street with the rusty blue Nissan sports car. "Maybe it's you I have a beef with. Sit up."

Izabel sat up and wiped the grit of sleep from her eyes. Her thin hair escaped from her ponytail in wisps. The rooster was the reason she'd been so tired.

He said, "Do I take that to be a yes, it is your bird?"

She shook her head. If she wasn't careful, anyone could see the way she felt about anything. She set her face to give nothing away—to ape the blank, resolute look her mother wore.

"That rooster goes off one more morning before the sun is up, and I'm going to call the cops on you and your mother, and they're gonna wring that bastard bird's neck."

She and her mother needed the rooster. But if the man called the police, they could be deported. No way was she going to tell her mother. Since Lina had enlisted, their mother hadn't been herself. When Izabel had told her about the three Brazilian men from up the block who'd been visited by the INS and later in the week hadn't come home from their landscaping job, Mamãe had closed her eyes and dropped her chin, closing Izabel right out. With her arms crossed over her chest, her voice clenched, Mamãe had said, "*Se voce nao se comportar eles vao me mandar para Brasilia.*" You don't behave, and they'll send us back, too.

Mamãe said the word "Brasilia" with an edge that made Izabel fear it.

The meat-faced man didn't usually come outside except to get into his Nissan and drive away. Izabel didn't think of him as one of the regulars on the street; those were the mail carrier, the old Greek men on the corner who leaned their chairs back against the crumbling retaining wall and coughed, and a little yellow dog Izabel called Cameron Diaz.

Her neighborhood in Lowell wasn't the kind that had trees. A refrigerator on its side obstructed one sidewalk. On the other, someone had collected statues made of concrete: a Madonna, a fishing boy, a fat little girl in a frilly dress, and some pineapples—each as big as a trashcan—chained and padlocked together so no one would steal them.

Cameron Diaz trotted past just then, too busy to pay attention to Izabel or to the chickens that clucked and peered at him through the fence. He headed for the black Cadillac with the crushed vinyl top that had been parked in the same spot two houses down for as long as Izabel could remember. The car slumped toward the curb on two flat tires. Cameron Diaz lifted his leg on it every day.

Izabel made a peeping sound and some of the hens tilted their eyes at her. The rooster had worn the feathers off their necks where he grabbed them and held them down. Their raw pink skin made Izabel's stomach whispery and hot, like the sad feeling before you throw up. She said, "How are we going to get him to shut up?" Which was enough to send the hens clucking and fleeing around the corner of the house.

Izabel's mother supplied eggs to the market at the bottom of Belvidere Hill, where people would pay more than four dollars a dozen for their eggs to be fresh and fertile from free-ranging chickens. Izabel's small house had no range to speak of. A chainlink fence hugged all of it but the stoop, leaving just enough room for the chickens to run. They laid their eggs wherever they could—in the weeds, in cracked flowerpots, in an upended hubcap, under the scrawny bushes.

The rooster marched arrogantly, his beauty in the long coppery feathers fanning out across his back and breast. Every morning as Izabel collected the eggs for her mother, he attacked her, enraged by her red sneakers. When she stepped anywhere near him, he would drop one wing like a cape, and come at her sideways, going for blood.

Izabel had barely left the stoop all summer, because she was waiting for the green card, and for the letter from her father that would finally tell them he was coming. Every Saturday evening, when Mamãe finished cleaning old Mrs. Burroughs's big house, she walked down to the bodega with the flashing red sign, *Sigue Corp, Effectivo en minutos, Envios a Mexico, Centro y Sud America*, where she fished the twenty dollar bills out of her big black handbag and wired the money to Brazil.

Izabel's father's letters came *correio*, airmail, months apart, as thin and tattered as moth wings. In the last one, he'd said it wouldn't be long now. He'd gone back to Brazil when his mother was dying. Though he said he took the mountain train all the way from Cantogallo to the U.S. Consulate every week, he hadn't been able to get back into the United States legally. Mamãe said she would die of shame and worry if he tried to come like a convict through the back door of Mexico with a "coyote." He'd been gone so long Izabel couldn't remember anything about him except that he'd painted houses, and up close, he'd smelled faintly like the vanilla cake her mother used to make.

If Izabel wasn't dancing or playing on the stoop, the mail carrier left the mail on the top step. Then it blew around in the wind and got stuck against the chainlink fence. Anything could happen to it. The mailbox was jammed full of electric bills. Her Mamãe had never had a key.

The stoop was where things happened, so waiting there wasn't so hard. Izabel made up routines, using the stair steps like the dancers on the Grammys. She dreamt of being as famous as Jennifer Lopez. While she waited for her friend Rupert to call down to her that *The Young and the Restless* was on or for her mother to come home, she kept strange dogs from worrying the chickens and invented games to play with a bouncing ball. Before they had enlisted, Rupert's brother Silverio used to kiss her sister Lina—sometimes with his tongue—while they sat right there on the bottom step.

Three days before, another visitor had come to the house. She knew how long it had been, because Rupert hadn't spoken to her since. She'd been watching a fat brown spider make a web on the corner of the step. While the spider's pointy fat ass touched down, there and there, with the almost invisible lines of sticky web attaching at angles as straight as street corners, a man in uniform stopped to chat with the old Greek men on the corner. Izabel had been too busy being close-up to a mystery to notice him. She couldn't decide whether the spider's work was the good kind of mystery, like the miraculous sound of her sister singing, or if it was more like when she looked at the nails going into Jesus' hands on the crucifix above the couch.

The officer passed the other cramped houses like theirs—shoehorned in and surrounded with tarmac and chainlink. He wore a freshly ironed green military uniform like the ones with the pins and ribbons the recruiters wore at the mall. She didn't know he was there until he put his foot on the bottom step.

The officer pulled a piece of paper out of his pocket and checked it against the street numbers. He had clear brown eyes and looked clean, as if he had been scrubbed pink from top to bottom with a scouring brush.

Thinking he'd come to deliver Lina's green card, Izabel stood up. The recruiters had told Lina that if she became a citizen soldier with the National Guard, the government would fast-track her application for citizenship starting with the work permit. Lina and Silverio had enlisted the day after they graduated from high school.

The officer said, "Is there a Darcia Araújo who lives here?" He didn't know how to pronounce Rupert's mother's name, got pinker, looked at her.

"She lives upstairs. Do you want me to get her?"

"No. No." The officer spoke very slowly and gently the way people do when they don't want to wake a baby. "Is there a doorbell?"

"It doesn't work."

"Well, then." He held the address on his knee as if he didn't know quite how he should stand. "Could I trouble you to get her?"

Izabel hopped down to the sidewalk and bellowed, "Rupert!"

Rupert, almost a whole year younger than she was, appeared at the window like a short pope come to bless the masses.

"Get your mother!"

The officer asked Izabel, "Does she speak English?"

"Not really."

"Can you translate?"

Rupert's mother, tall and pillowy, with a saggy soft face, opened the door partway. Red lipstick made her lips seem huge and loose.

The officer asked, "Darcia Araújo?" He took his hat off and held it in his hands in front of him. "The mother of Silverio Araújo?" Izabel translated what he said.

Darcia nodded and kept her eyes fastened on his face while she let the door go behind her. Mamãe appeared like a shadow near the downstairs window.

"I am Army National Guard Notification Officer Constantine Kritikos." Izabel turned the words into Portuguese. "I am sorry to report that your son was wounded in a roadside attack yesterday in Fallujah."

Darcia wrapped her hands up tight in her apron.

Officer Kritikos said, "He was medevacked to a hospital in Germany."

Izabel suddenly couldn't speak. The words felt like bees on her tongue, fuzzy and dangerous. She remembered Silverio closing his eyes as he kissed Lina. She felt her heart thumping and couldn't say a thing. Rupert stared at her from the shadows of the vestibule. He shambled shyly out onto the top step next to his mother and asked the officer, "What is medevacked?"

Officer Kritikos explained about the helicopter. Izabel's tongue felt too big for her mouth.

Rupert looked quickly at Izabel and began to translate for his mother. His nose was running, and the soft skin between his eyes puckered.

Izabel did not cry. More than anything, she wanted to be important in this.

"Within the week, I should have word on his condition." Officer Kritikos saw the confusion on Rupert's face and corrected himself. "I'll tell you how he's doing as soon as I know."

Rupert started to translate, but Izabel couldn't stand the sound of his little boy voice.

When the officer said, "Your son Silverio is a good soldier," both Izabel and Rupert said, "*Seu filho Silverio . . .*" She narrowed her eyes at Rupert and turned red. She drowned him out, "He was following orders. His commanding officer reported that Private Araújo's Humvee was leading a transport column. He couldn't have done anything differently or better than he was doing it. You should be proud."

Darcia's smudged lipstick made her look like she couldn't take care of the simplest thing. Rupert stared glumly at Izabel, whose voice had won out, and jutted his jaw. Darcia blinked and wrapped and unwrapped her hands in her apron. She said "thank you" to the officer as if her voice came through layers of cloth.

Officer Kritikos put his hat back on his head and said he was sorry. He'd be back when he had more news. Mamãe stepped out quietly and led Darcia back inside, as if Rupert's mother was suddenly very old.

The night after the officer's visit, Izabel had fallen asleep on the fold-out she shared with her mother, holding Mamãe's fragile wooden music box to her ear. Mamãe had fished it out of the trash when she cleaned at Mrs. Burroughs's house. It had a red stripe across the top. It whirred and plinked a tiny tune while Darcia cried upstairs.

Izabel woke later to the smell of steam and starch, to a rhythmic thudding, coming from the kitchen. The kitchen light sliced at an angle across the mattress. She sat up to see her mother standing at the ironing board pressing all the clothes Lina had left behind. The clock said 3:05. One by one, Mamãe pulled shirts and shorts and skirts out of a pile, sprayed them, shuttled the iron over them purposefully, rocking her weight into the motion, then folded them onto the neat stack on the table.

Just before Lina'd left, Mamãe had reached up and released each of Lina's silver hoop earrings into her work-worn hand. Lina said, "Mãe. Mãe. What are you doing?"

Her mother didn't answer, but carried the earrings to the bathroom, where she took her toothbrush and toothpaste and polished each one, working up a gray, pasty lather across her fingertips and thumb. She rinsed the earrings, rubbed them with a corner of towel, and tried to put them, shining, back in Lina's soft brown earlobes. Lina frowned and put them in herself.

Izabel would have let Mãe do it. Just to feel her mother's fingers on her skin. She fell back to sleep to the rhythm of her mother's hands with the heavy iron, thumping and pressing, creasing Lina's seams straight.

If the rooster crowed during the night after the neighbor complained, Izabel didn't hear it. She was so tired she slept through her mother's leaving in the morning. She had forgotten the rooster and was inventing a dance on the stoop when Rupert stuck his face out the upstairs window.

He said, "You are waiting for nothing."

She put her hand up to shade her view.

He hadn't forgotten who'd won out translating Officer Kritikos's words. His mouth twisted up on one side as it did when he hated the taste of his dinner and was going to slide as much as he could into the kitchen table drawer when the mothers weren't looking. He said, "Your father isn't ever coming."

"So you say."

"My mother said."

"How does she know?"

"My mother said he's bought a house and started a new family by now with all the money your mother sends him."

"You don't know anything." Izabel fought to still her face. "That's not what I'm waiting for, anyway."

"Then what?"

"I'm waiting for the green card."

"That green card isn't going to do *you* any good."

"Not *me*. My mother."

"A green card only works for the person whose name is on it. My mother *has* one." Rupert had been born in the United States. Izabel had been born early, before they could get out of Brazil, ruining her mother's chance for a green card. Rupert's citizenship was the only advantage he had over her. She bent to tie her shoe so he couldn't see her face. What if he was right? If he had been next to her, she would have punched him fast, one-two, right in his soft face.

She heard him clump down the stairs inside. The door opened a teasing, tiny bit. Rupert put his mouth to the crack. "This morning the rusty Nissan guy told me he's going to call the landlord and tell him about your rooster, so maybe you *are* going to see your father." He shut the door and held it so that no matter how she threw her weight into pulling it open, the most she could get was a crack—just enough for him to let out the words "back in Brazil." She got so mad she almost forced the door open.

Then suddenly, the resistance was gone and it swung wide with her effort. Rupert thumped up the stairs as fast as he could go. She would trip him and pin his arms and spit in his face.

She reached to stop him slamming the upstairs door. The noise of the door on her fingers was worse than her screaming afterward. Rupert bent over catching his breath, telling her he was sorry again and again. She wasn't listening.

He got some ice in a plastic bag for her, like the nurse at school, and then stood at the end of the couch where she curled in a ball. He startled when she reached for the ice.

She waited for the cold ache to replace the pain from the door and for her shaking hatred of him to be replaced by something else. A mockingbird next door imitated the sound of Mrs. Moriarty's pulley clothesline. Rupert stared at her fingers as if that could make them feel better. A plane flew over. Someone on the next block shouted, "Hey, Sully!"

Who else did they have all day, but one another?

Later, after her fingers had quit throbbing, Izabel called up to Rupert from the stoop, "If you help me catch the rooster, I'll let you have a sniff of the shampoo Lina left behind." He had a crush on Lina that no one was supposed to know about.

They waited until after supper when Mamãe and Darcia were busy cleaning up.

Izabel lowered herself into the chicken run, being careful to avoid getting snagged on the mean twists of metal at the top of the fence. Rupert balanced on the fence corner, wearing his Shaq jersey, ready for his cue. The heat of the day had stuck around and was rising from the tarmac. A basketball bounced over and over in the court on the next block.

The rooster strutted around the side of the house. Izabel danced side to side, kicking up her bright red high-tops, her ribs and her belly button showing between her top and her shorts. She whispered so her mother—behind the curtained kitchen window, washing the dishes and singing a hymn in her deep quavery voice—wouldn't catch on to what she was doing.

"I hate you, rooster; come and get me. Get me. Get me, Roostah! Come and get me, Roostah man." The bird eyed her sneakers and made threatening moves with his bill. The feathers around his neck leapt and shimmered. She filled up with a mysterious feeling, as strong and hot and pure as sunlight—maybe as sure as faith—that if she could trap him, if she could truly shut up the rooster, her sister would get home safe.

When the rooster wobbled his comb and flashed his gold eyes, she took off so fast she was flying, down through the bulkhead door—with the rooster flashing his crazy quick legs after her. Rupert clanged the metal door closed after them. A second later, Izabel, who'd taken the stairs up two at a time inside, shut the kitchen door, and the rooster was in the basement.

Izabel, breathless and flushed with victory, met Rupert out front with Lina's bottle of shampoo in her hand. She said, "That will do it. It's pretty dark down there. He won't bother that man until I let him loose again in the morning." She slapped him five.

They sat on the stoop, listening to a cat fight somewhere up toward Hosford Square. Cameron Diaz clicked past like the busybody he was. Izabel said, "Ready?"

Rupert closed his eyes. His face was the color of toffee candy, like an

Indian prince. She flipped the cap open and held the coconut shampoo under his nose. He breathed deeply. The smell of Lina's hair came rolling out of the bottle, certain and sweet. It surprised Izabel, stunned her into stillness.

The deal with Rupert had been only one sniff, but she was too taken over by the smell to care when he took the bottle from her and breathed again and again. Sometimes when she was falling asleep, her sister's singing came into her head clear and sharp as glass. Lina would sing as she walked Izabel to the mall on Saturdays while their mother cleaned old Mrs. Burroughs's spooky house on Belvidere Hill.

Wherever Lina went, she sang. Lina's singing made Izabel's scalp tingle, and she felt like she might float right up in the air, lifted by the sound the way she used to think her kite could lift her. Lina sang songs from church, from MTV, the radio, ads like the one for Mattress Giant: "If you want that ooh aah feel, come to Mattress Giant. If you want the ooh aah deal, we got the best prices. Only at Mattress Giant. Ooh. Aah." People would turn toward her voice, and Lina would look out from under her thick bangs. Everyone said she could have won American Idol without even trying. Even though Izabel herself couldn't carry a tune, she wanted to puff up and strut when, just to hear her sister, people rolled down their car windows or paused on the step as they boarded the #11 bus.

Smelling the shampoo, Izabel listened for her sister's voice but couldn't hear it. That night, when she crawled in by Mamãe on the fold-out couch and lay very still, she left the music box unwound under her pillow, hoping Lina would sing in her head.

The rooster crowed at 4:30 A.M. His noise penetrated the furnace conduits and cockadoodle-dooed through the vent in the floor, startling Izabel awake. She found herself bent up with her feet pressed against Mãe's solid hip and thigh as if she were trekking up her mother's side.

The humid night held Mamãe's sleep-breath close. She didn't move after she fell asleep, even when the rooster crowed as loudly as if he were in the room with them. She lay on her back with her rough brown hands hanging on to one another across the top of her old striped housedress. Even in sleep, her mouth didn't relax.

Izabel slipped off the mattress and shoved one of the couch pillows over the air vent. She had thought she'd won because their neighbor wouldn't hear the rooster anymore. But there was a vent in every room in their little house. That bird had probably woken Rupert and his mother.

She sat very still on the edge of the mattress. Until Lina left, Mãe had taken care of almost everything. She might still know what to do to about the neighbor and his threat. Izabel reached her hand for Mãe's shoulder. She gently laid her hand on the worn fabric of the housedress close to where the cloth met Mãe's skin.

But her Mãe's face looked closed—shut tight as a box. Izabel thought of the dry cracks running through the fragile wooden music box, and took her hand back. Mãe, brittle, scared her more than the neighbor man.

She lay down, not touching her mother, and tried to be still. She thought of Lina in that desert country wearing camo like the troops on the news. She thought of her sister having to keep quiet—and her mouth went dry as sand.

The next morning, Izabel decided to leave the rooster locked up until after she had collected the eggs. She dropped into the yard, for once not need-ing to worry about him, and there he was, a chaos of feathers, bruising her shins with his wings and feet and jabbing her ankle with his thick yellow bill. He was too fast for her. She kicked hard enough to kill him, and connected with nothing but air. Her only escape was to climb the fence.

She balanced at the top. He'd broken skin. Her thin sock bloomed with blood just above her sneaker.

The rooster strutted and paused, pecked at the dirt, and worked his way, king of his yard, around the corner.

Her skin felt too small to hold her in. She might rip right open with fury. She pressed her hands hard against the fence's metal twists. She pressed until her hands hurt more than her ankle and she could breathe again.

She let herself down slowly to the packed dirt of the chicken run. The broody hen laid her eggs in the upturned hubcap by the front. Quickly, gently, Izabel slid her shaking hand under the hen. Her feathers were soft and smelly, and hot. Izabel searched under the bushes for the other eggs, keeping her eye out for the rooster. He was going after the hens, grabbing any he could catch, and mating. She scooped the last egg from a broken plastic flowerpot.

Inside, she found her mother standing at the kitchen counter next to the egg boxes, buttering *bolos levedos*. "*Como o galo entrou para dentro de casa?*"

Izabel pulled guava paste and cheese from the fridge. "The rooster isn't inside."

Her mother took the basket to the sink and began, slowly, to wipe the dirt and stray feathers from each egg with a fresh cloth. "Izabel?"

With her mouth full of bun and guava paste and cheese, Izabel asked, "Why are you asking me?"

Mamãe stopped what she was doing and raised her head. She didn't speak English but she understood it well enough. Izabel crossed her legs so her mother couldn't see the blood. Too late. An egg-shaped lump was starting above her anklebone.

Disapproval rose off her mother like fumes. "You drive me crazy." "*Voce me deixa doida.*" Why can't you do the simplest thing right?

The lump had a perfect little red hole in the middle. A bullet hole might look the same, only bigger.

Her mother said, "Take off those stupid red shoes. How many times do I have to tell you? It's your own fault he attacks you. Then go apologize to Darcia for waking her in the middle of the night. With all she's going through."

After the mothers had gone to work, Izabel took her mind off things by moving like a silver star, from point to point, down the steps, then quick and round, like a ball, a bouncing girl, off the wall and into the air. She felt best when she was in motion, when moving and thinking at once. She would never take off her sneakers. Lina had bought them for her at Foot Locker the day she enlisted. Sometimes when the WLWL traffic helicopter hovered over the Lowell Connector, Izabel would think how her sneakers might be the only bright spot from Hosford Square to the laundromat, and maybe all the way down Gorman through the Bleachery and across the canal to where the bright flags flew at the Mile of Mills Mall. She landed on the sidewalk and brought herself upright to see a police officer sliding out of his cruiser next to the chained statues. He stood on the far side of his car. Had the meat-faced neighbor called? How could you tell an INS officer from any other kind?

She tried to make the look on her face as smooth and sturdy as pavement. No chickens were in sight. She pretended she was going inside, just a hungry girl on summer vacation whose mother had called her in for lunch.

From the shadows of the vestibule, she watched as he took out a pad of paper and wrote on it, using the top of his cruiser as a desk. He ripped the paper off and came toward the house. Izabel ducked. He'd see her the second he started up the steps. But he walked down the sidewalk and stuck the paper, a ticket, under the windshield-wiper of the smashed-in Cadillac with the flat tires. She didn't believe she was safe until he'd gotten back into his car and pulled away.

Late that afternoon, when Notification Officer Constantine Kritikos strode down Keene Street, Izabel saw him coming. She watched his walk the way she would watch her mother's, searching for lightness, for a turn of a shoulder or softness around his mouth that would mean he brought something other than bad news. He carried a folder under one arm and swung the other.

She didn't know him well enough to read him, and she didn't really know how to pray. She stuck both red sneakers out in front of her and concentrated on them. While whispering Lina's name, Izabel quickly tied each with a double knot so there could be no doubt, and waited for him.

"Hello, again," he said. "Is Mrs. Araújo home?" He was wearing silver sunglasses.

"Not yet." She could barely look at him because the sun was right by his head.

"Are you expecting her?"

"They're usually home by now." She held her hand up to block the sun. She tried to look somewhere else.

He gave a little tug on his pant leg above the knee and put his foot on the bottom step. "Would you mind if I waited here with you?"

"Is Silverio dead?"

"No. He is healing."

"You can wait." If she made herself look at him despite the sun, she could see herself in his lenses, two tiny versions of herself, her pink shirt, aqua shorts, red sneakers.

He took his glasses off and held them out to her. "Here, you want to borrow these? You look like a deer in the headlights."

She shook her head. She couldn't tell whether she wanted to be nice to him or not. "What does that mean, deer in the headlights?"

Officer Kritikos explained that a strong light would confuse and paralyze an animal at night. "Our soldiers doing house-to-house night searches use their powerful headlamps to help intimidate the enemy."

Rupert pushed open the front door and sidled out next to them. His shirt was too small, the stripes all stretched and riding up.

Mamãe and Darcia turned the corner by the laundromat just then, coming from the bus. Seeing them coming home eased something in Izabel, as if she'd been holding her breath. Mamãe, short and square, stayed close to the buildings, as invisible as possible—as if she weren't hauling anything so obvious as a vacuum cleaner. Pear-shaped Darcia carried the hose and attachments.

Officer Kritikos didn't stay long. He told them Silverio was lucky. He was mending. He had lost his left hand and was in a hospital in Germany where soldiers learned to use prosthetic limbs.

That night, the children took cover in the corner where the trashcans were stored, where dark had saturated the yard. They were supposed to be asleep. Even with their hands out in front of them, every step felt like they might fall into the deep darkness. Izabel forced her eyes as wide as they would go, but it didn't help.

Someone laughed in the boardinghouse next door. Then there was the sound of a slap, and a woman giggled. Izabel's eyes slowly adjusted. She could make out the fence, the side of the house.

Rupert had brought his special flashlight from the Utuadeña Market. It was shaped like a credit card. All you did was pinch it on the market logo and it lit. He handed it to Izabel and took his post by the trashcan. He held the lid poised.

Izabel whispered fiercely, "When you do it, watch out for my *fingers*."

Rupert said, "Very funny. Ha. Ha." One of the hens clucked. Both children froze.

Izabel tested the flashlight. If her plan didn't work, the night would erupt with more noise than the meat-faced neighbor had ever heard on Keene Street.

She shined the light directly at the fence where the rooster usually slept. He'd wilted there and looked small, but he pulled his head up and opened his near eye as she came for him, the light in her teeth. He lit up, his comb vivid, his shawl of copper feathers glimmering. Everything else fell away in murky shadow. The black part of his eye closed to a pinpoint, making his eye as gold as anything in church.

Izabel grabbed him. His body felt harder than the hens', his feathers silkier. He waved his head like a snake trying to focus past the light. His comb stood upright. If she could only get him into the trashcan, if Rupert could be quick with the lid, they could keep him in the dark until the next morning after the neighbor man had driven away in his car. The crack in the lid would let in a little air. Even if he crowed, the sound would be muffled.

She held tight, spreading her fingers wide and pinning his wings to his sides. With the effort, her teeth let up on the flashlight button. The whole yard collapsed into darkness. He began to struggle. She held him and his flailing feet as far away from her face as she could. His bill was thick and greenish in the dark. She concentrated to keep holding on. She bit down, turning the brilliant, narrow beam on him again.

The brightness zapped him into submission. His legs lost everything and hung limp. His wings conformed to her hands. His head sank on his neck. He blinked, defeated.

She clamped that rooster's wings to his sides, and kept biting down. If she could do this, if she could just do this. Holding the bird out, his legs dangling, she raced, a blinding blaze of will, toward Rupert and the silencing dark of the trashcan.

Luck Be a Lady

FRENCHIE DURAS, WHO LIVED ALONE WITH HIS SECRETS, DID NOT WANT TO be found dead with the bone in his shirt pocket. Anyone finding it on him would think it was gruesome, and he hated the idea of someone getting it so wrong. No one but Stella would understand his carrying a secret reminder of her in his left front pocket. She'd like the irony, after the way they used to tear off their clothes, that now he had to fold his shirt carefully at the end of the day so as not to send all that remained of her skidding across his bedroom floor.

Frenchie wore soft wool shirts, one on top of the other, hiding how his chest protruded like a bird's. His white hair swept back from a brow that looked fragile—something he had never been. His hands were too big for him now and hung from big-boned arms that had been powerful. He'd known, from the long uneven pauses between his heartbeats and from the way he listed unexpectedly to one side when he walked from his bathroom to his kitchen, that he didn't have long. The results of his latest tests, which he'd received that morning, told him it was time to call Kaylene, the girl who drove for him. His heart had tripled in size.

Frenchie's secrets kept him separate. He wouldn't mind leaving most of them behind—like the cash in the magazine pockets of his La-Z-Boy.

When he was gone and his furniture auctioned off, some joker would hit the jackpot. Likewise the stash of silver dollars in the false-bottomed drawer in his kitchen.

He had different plans for Stella's bone.

⌒

Many years ago, Frenchie used to drive around Lowell on Sundays with his wife, Martine, just for something to do. After she got too sick, he drove alone. That was how he'd found the stone wall to work on. Frost deep in the ground had thrown the stones from their purpose and left them strewn at the border of meadow and woods. He didn't know who owned the land. On his days off, in all kinds of weather, he'd sweat to rebuild some long-dead farmer's ruined work.

He would fit his hands to the stones, feel their rough curves, test their heft, eye their thickness, the contours, and snug them against each other. His focus made him forget the field behind and the woods in front of him, until his back ached. Then he'd notice the birds that had been singing all along, and the occasional car passing on the road below. Working surrounded by the careless beauty of the earth's business helped him find the patience he needed to live the rest of his life.

Three or four years into his wall rebuilding, a young woman carrying a handbag strode up from the road through the tall grass and meadow-sweet. She wore polka-dotted high heels, but by the time she reached him, a heel had broken off, and she walked unevenly.

He recognized her from the Phoenix Luncheonette, the place he owned—and where he worked the rest of the week. She put her broken heel on the wall and opened her handbag. "I didn't know what you wanted me to do with this." She held a wad of bills out to him. The sleeves of her dress rippled in the breeze that lifted across the field.

"I didn't think I'd be seeing that again," he said.

"Did you think I was going to take off with it?"

"I would have."

She looked him up and down, taking in his sturdy build, the stone dust on his pants, and said, "I doubt that." She held it out to him. He didn't take it.

He'd brought a thermos of strong coffee and poured her a cup. She dropped the roll of bills back into her handbag. "Thanks. They said I'd find you here on Sundays." She looked at his work. "Is this a second job?" She sipped her coffee.

He said, "I don't need that money."

A gust of wind pinned her dress against her legs. She eyed him steadily, "Is there something wrong with it?"

"Same as any money: there's funny business behind every bill."

"That doesn't usually stop people from wanting it." She reached into her handbag. "If it isn't yours, tell me who to take it to. It's burning a hole in my purse."

"It's yours."

She bounced the wad of cash, testing its heft in her hand. "Do you know how much is here?" Her nails were lacquered brilliant red.

He'd made a split-second decision and thrown the money her way because she looked like someone who wouldn't do anything stupid. Now he turned back to his work, heaved a big, uneven stone onto the wall, and shimmed it into place with a smaller one.

She finished her coffee, and fitted the heel to her shoe experimentally.

There was something sad and dashing about her standing with her dress flapping like a flag at the edge of the woods, but he didn't know what made him say he didn't need the money. Maybe he wanted to seem the sort of man who had plenty.

He worked the counter of his luncheonette, short order from 5:30 in the morning until 6 at night except Sundays and Christmas. At home, he fixed supper for his wife, who was nearly housebound. They ate, watching TV in the bedroom until she tired and fell asleep. The bills for her care piled up on the table in the hallway.

After he had swiveled the big stone to fit better, he couldn't keep from turning to look at the woman. She sat on the grass behind him with her dress tucked under her legs, smoking a cigarette. Beyond her, the sunlight glinted off the mills, the bridges over the Merrimack and Concord rivers, and the dome of city hall.

Her hair was dark, almost black, and stylish. He watched her red nails lift a speck, maybe tobacco, from the end of her tongue. Her skin, to touch, might be the world's opposite of stone.

"I'm waiting to hear what strings are attached," she said.

He shook his head and pointed the way she had come. She slid the bangles on her wrist up and down. "I came all the way up here to return it." She took her other shoe off and stood stocking-footed in the grass.

He didn't want to have to think; he wanted simply for her to understand the money was hers and to get out of his sight.

She said, "How about if we start over?" She gave him a wry, off-center smile. "Then we'll know that if you're going to do anything stupid, at least you've had time to think about it." She stuck the heel of her good shoe between two rocks in the wall and pried it off as if she were opening a bottle of beer. She dropped both heels into her bag, put her shoes on, and left him. He watched her go, unbelieving at first, and then fed up with himself.

What did she think he was going to think about? Every workday, Frenchie left his house in the quiet of early morning, crossed Central Street, and let himself in the luncheonette's back door. He always used the same pull-and-turn to open it. He flipped on the lights, lifted a fresh apron from the drawer and tied the strings comfortably low around his hips. He turned on the grill and washed his hands, took papers of bacon out of the walk-in and started prepping the onions. Every day was a blur of orders and faces, most of them well known to him. At 5:45, he counted the day's take and walked home to his wife's suffering, his dread.

What was there to consider, really? The antiseptic smell of his house, Martine's blood-testing kit spilling out of its case on her bedside table, the mess in the kitchen that waited until he got to it? How he could hardly remember the flirty, unpredictable girl he'd married? Her trim little body. Her smart mouth. How she used to keep him off-balance, intrigued.

Love had brought him straight to the disappointment of a narrow life.

He started after the young woman but couldn't see where she'd gone.

He'd let that money out of his hands a second time, and it felt as if he'd stolen it directly from his wife's well-being. And what for? For a sense of importance, to be someone who made grand gestures to a beautiful woman? He didn't even know her name. Any savvy he'd thought was his had been tossed into the rubbish the minute she'd found him working on the wall.

During the next week, he asked around. By the next Sunday, when she climbed back up the hill, he knew her name was Stella Lewis, that she'd come from up north and gotten mixed up in some union boosting or busting (depending on who you asked) at one of the mills. She had no family.

That day, as he worked on the wall, his mind didn't so much empty as it filled with the shapes of the stones in his hands. Rebuilding made sense to something inside him that craved the lifting, the fitting, the eventual tiredness. Each stone that fit brought the satisfaction of a solution. Fifty feet or more now stood mended. That wall was the place in his life he made progress.

This time, she wore flat shoes. She didn't look him in the eye. She didn't carry a handbag. She turned to the view as if she'd suddenly gone shy. She stared at her hands, at her nails, then tried putting them behind her back. She asked, "Do you have a cigarette?"

His problem wasn't just that she was such a pleasure to look at. She'd put herself together with attention. She knew how to compensate for the discrepancies between how one is and how one looks. He handed her a cigarette. She let him light it for her.

She held her mouth to the side to exhale the smoke. "I saw the paper."

He turned away from her. The *Lowell Sun* had written up the charges against him and how there hadn't been enough evidence to substantiate the claims of the state cops.

He said, "You've decided something?"

"It's your money."

He turned to her. "But you didn't bring it with you."

She folded her arms. "What would you say if I told you I'd put it in the bank?"

"I'd say," he pursed his lips and shrugged, "that would be the evidence."

"The story in the paper is true?"

He pressed his lips together. His arrest had embarrassed him deeply.

"It's not in the bank," she said. "But it's safe."

He patted the top of the wall by him. "Come and sit." He was looking for something not to like about her. "Let's see if this wall of mine is worth anything."

At the time, he had no notion of how important the place would become to him. The view of Lowell wasn't half bad from there. The mile of mills took up most of the horizon.

"What would you do with eleven and some thousand dollars?" he said.

Her eyes lightened up, and she might have been about to smile.

"I can see you in a fur coat," he said.

She laughed and dabbed at the perspiration on her forehead with the back of her hand. "Not today." Her bracelets jingled. "I'd invest, but not in that."

"Then what?"

She cocked her head at him. "Who wants to know?"

"I'm Frenchie."

"I know that, but so is every Tom, Dick, and Harry in Little Canada. And the rest of them haven't been thinking about giving me thousands of dollars."

"My name is Robert Duras."

"Robert Duras." She looked at the sky. "You want me to keep my mouth shut about what happened at the Phoenix. So you think it's a good idea to let me have the money, especially if I didn't ask for more."

He said, "It's more complicated than that." She had a tiny white scar on her chin shaped like a chevron.

"Everything is," she said. "Neither of us wants to owe the other. What if we both put it to use?"

"Split it?"

"How about a partnership?"

He hadn't understood just what she had in mind, but in all the years

Frenchie had been taking bets over the counter at the Phoenix, he'd never allowed anyone to find a way into his business. Disgusted with his own sloppiness, he'd eased himself off the wall and said, "Just keep the cash."

⌒

After the morning rush, Wednesday, a few weeks before, he'd handed old Mr. DeLisle his usual orange juice. "No Donuts O'Neill," the cop who'd put four bucks for his mother on Minnie Mouse to show in the seventh, read the comics to whoever would listen. Frank Sinatra's latest hit played on the radio.

Dot, the weaver, sucked on her cigarette and slid ten dollars across the counter toward Frenchie. He scraped down the grill. The sun, coming in the side window, lit up the saltine tins he'd flattened to make the grill's backsplash. He whistled with the radio, ". . . the best that I can do is pray . . ." Luck had been a lady the day before. He'd had a hunch on the big race at Suffolk Downs, and he'd played it. He was flush—which turned out to be the problem.

Dot said, "'Genie's Dream' to win in the fifth." She'd studied the cheat sheet ever since he opened. She had four teeth left, all up front. She squinted at him through her dusty glasses and said, "This ten is the one that's going to make you rip up my IOU."

He took her money. The last time she'd gotten behind with him, she'd had her nephew drop a case of men's irregular socks at the Phoenix, and she'd called it even. Gifts like that stuffed the basement: boxes of 25-watt light bulbs, a carton of sanitary napkins, two cases of plumber's candles, a full-length men's coat in calf skin.

Old Mr. DeLisle looked a little peaked, so Frenchie poured him a cup of coffee. He liked to throw in a little extra that no one had asked for, a BLT or a cherry Coke, for which he wouldn't charge. He'd learned to keep everyone just a little indebted to him. He'd made his way from nothing, the kid of unlucky immigrants who lived and died working the mills. He'd come to run the Phoenix by falling for Martine, whose father had established the place. Busy at the grill, he heard what was shared among his customers until he knew all about them. They thought, because of his easy way with them, that they knew all about him, too. He fed them, always a little more than they asked for, and every time he did, he made a little more room for himself, a few more favors, and a little more privacy right there in their midst.

The state police stepped up to the counter like anyone else, except they had the jodhpurs and boots and towered over everyone there. When they asked to speak privately with Frenchie, they surprised Officer O'Neill as much as Dot.

"There isn't really anywhere to talk except in the walk-in," Frenchie said.

They didn't seem to see anything amusing in that. He wiped his hands on his apron and showed them to the cooler door. They had to duck. He caught O'Neill's eye and made as if to shut the big dopes in. O'Neill would have given one of his snorting laughs, but nothing like this had ever happened before.

The sergeant did the talking. He remained polite and businesslike, surrounded by boxes of lard and bottles of milk, with Frenchie leaning against a shelf of lettuce and cabbage heads. Frenchie's brain sped up; he could feel it catch and purr. The colors on the food labels seemed extraordinarily vivid; the cops' buttons and badges shone. He put his hands in his pockets in case they shook. The sergeant finished with, "We hope you won't mind coming down to the city station."

Frenchie had friends at the station. "Have a look around here first, if you want." Dot or one of the others would have hidden the cigar box of betting slips he kept on the counter by the napkin dispenser.

His pocket bulged with cash, making his hips look wider than they were. He opened the walk-in door. The sergeant indicated that he should go first, so he put one foot out and took a chance on holding the door for them. They went for it.

He smelled the coffee burning, and except for the disappearance of the telltale cigar box, and the appearance at the counter of the woman whose shoes and handbag matched, it looked like no one had moved. She sat on the stool closest to the walk-in, wearing a little hat with fake cherries on it, like something out of a fashion magazine. The radio sang, "It's so easy when you use Lestoil," and that's when he tripped.

He couldn't say what made him choose her, exactly. He hadn't had a lot of time. He faked a fall, as if the lip of the walk-in had caught his toe, and as he sprawled, he tossed the contents of his pocket at her feet.

Unlike the Statees, who didn't turn until they heard the thud of his fall, she saw the roll of money land. She lifted her handbag casually and set it down so the money couldn't be seen.

As the state cops helped Frenchie up, one on either arm, she dropped the roll of bills into her bag like a pack of cigarettes.

∽

Frenchie waited for Kaylene on the steps to the porch. He did not want her or anyone else seeing how much time he took to get down the stairs. Since his heart attack, moving winded him. The day Kaylene started driving for him, he'd been having the devil of a time backing out of a parking space at the Stop & Shop. People stopped to watch. Just the sort of nightmare he'd feared most about aging. She'd rested her bags on his window and said, "Hey Frenchie. Slide over." He'd known her since she was nine or ten and had been taken in by old Mr. DeLisle's daughter-in-law, June, who'd worked at Stella's salon. Kaylene probably just didn't want to have to carry her groceries home. She backed the car out like a pro.

Now, for the warm summer day, he wore a brushed flannel shirt. He chilled easily, and could only bear to have soft clothes next to his skin. He had bathed, and shaved, and combed what remained of his white hair straight back from his face. When she pulled up, he patted his pocket to be sure he had everything and walked out to his old white Dodge Aspen.

Kaylene opened the door for him from the inside and said, "The old Aspirin still rolls."

He was never sure what she was talking about. She used the trashiest words, half of them made up, and her voice was so husky for her size it surprised him still. He lowered himself into the seat and remembered that "the Aspirin" was Kaylene's nickname for the car, which he let her keep in return for helping him with errands.

"How are you, Frenchie?" Kaylene was young and silky. A fake diamond stud glinted in her belly button.

He remembered her as a little mite, twirling on the stools of the Phoenix, wearing pink cowgirl boots. "I'm old," he said. "But so far nothing's fallen off."

She changed her hair color quicker than a mink. That day she wore it strawberry blond and short. She worked as the colorist at A Cut Above. She claimed to have learned everything she knew from Stella. Kaylene's sharp little chin and ears stuck out. She leaned her arm on the back of the seat and sprawled, taking up a lot of space for someone so tiny. When she was a kid, she hung around the Phoenix, not exactly underfoot, but into everyone's business. He remembered her studying the racing forms and trying to make her elbows reach the counter so she could look like one of the regulars—like she belonged. She had a way of showing up when he didn't expect her, or anyone. When even he couldn't say where Stella was, Kaylene always knew.

Now, on her tight upper arm, she had a new tattoo, a swirly green *G*. To see a young one scarring herself up pained him. He knew how quickly just living would ruin her. She was too young to understand anything.

He had trouble with the seat belt, which embarrassed him. She leaned over to buckle him in, bringing the brisk, slightly chemical smells of anti-perspirant and chewing gum with her. "Where to?"

"You can't ask me about today."

She raised her eyebrows. Her hairstyle brought out the upward slant of her eyes. "Up to your old tricks?"

"Take me up Aiken Street to Route 113." He folded his hands in his lap. What did she know of his old tricks? He hadn't taken bets since his heart attack, which was more years ago than he cared to count, and no one knew about the bone that Rafferty, rest his soul, had held out of Stella's ashes for him. "I'm not doing anything that's going to get you in trouble."

"I'd risk it for you, you old coot."

He sat back and breathed. They passed two brown-skinned girls climbing onto a bus at the Keene Street intersection, the little one in red high tops, the older one singing loudly, beautifully, but Kaylene drove too fast for Frenchie to catch the words. "Where's the fire?" he asked. Kaylene was barely tall enough to see over the steering wheel. He leaned to check the speedometer.

"Trust me, Frenchie. Have I cracked up this car? Do you see one dent?"

On the dashboard, tiny ink footprints had been penned. They climbed over the hump of the radio and led to a pair of doll shoes—stiletto heels, perfect pointy toes—as if they'd just been kicked off, one tipped on its side.

She saw him looking. "I didn't do that to your car."

He reached to put the shoe upright. It was glued in place. "I won't stop you doing what you want."

"But I didn't." Kaylene pointed to the ceiling light. "I didn't do that either." The rocker switch had been changed to a pull chain, and from it dangled one small glittery red pump.

She said, "This has been going on for a couple of weeks. I leave the car locked, and when I come back to it, there are more Barbie slippers. It's scary. Last week, they were showered over it—all these tiny shoes, hundreds of fuck-me pumps the size of jujubes." She made a sprinkling gesture with her hand. "Red, green, blue, yellow, black. Strewn over the hood, the trunk, the bumpers."

"Love notes?"

"I think I might need your help."

Frenchie wasn't as interested as he knew he ought to be. "Those days are gone." In the old days, he would have called in a favor and found out which cracker box was messing with the car and why. Now he felt that what happened here, or what happened next, had nothing to do with him anymore. His life was behind him.

As she approached the Ouellette Bridge, he said, "I want to go to Grosvenor Hill."

"You mean up by Pheasant Circle?"

"No." He didn't know any Pheasant Circle. "I'll tell you where to leave me."

"Okay, Mister Mystiphistical."

Her manicured hands spun the wheel lightly. She took the turn too fast, and he braced himself against the door. She wore a thumb ring. She was so young and alien, really. Grandparents probably felt like this all the time. The world belonged to her now. To her, he might be nothing more than an old man too pathetic to do his own driving. When she let him out in the pullout at the bottom of his hill, he said, "Come for me in a couple of hours."

She said, "Don't you want me to wait?"

"No." Annoyance flickered in him—as if she were still that pesky little kid wanting something.

Thickets of poplar and willow, maybe twenty feet tall had completely overtaken what he'd known as open meadow. When he'd thought about climbing the hill to the wall, he pictured the field as it had always been: grasses and cow vetch, knee high; just as it had been when Stella first climbed it.

He stood by the side of the road and looked up at the thoroughness of green growth between him and where he knew the wall to be. He hadn't been here since Stella died. He wouldn't put odds on making it up that hill.

He'd considered taking her bone to the cemetery, or burying it in the roots of the little tree that grew through the sidewalk in front of the Phoenix, either of which might have made sense. But neither had felt right. As strange as his errand might seem, he knew that Stella would have liked his goal.

A car honked at him. Kaylene, still there, rolled down her window and pointed at the hill. He signaled impatiently for her to go along, turned his back, and stepped into the trees.

Someone had mown the field at least once after the trees began to grow, and those trees had come back, eight or twelve saplings to each stump. Frenchie pushed between the clumps into a closed world where the air felt thick and woolly. The trees pressed in on him. He held the sapling branches back and moved carefully, as he had done when hunting as a kid. The best part had been going quietly, surrounded by the small noises of a place where few people passed. Later, he'd found the same kind of pleasure in the solitude and physical demands of rebuilding the wall. He wondered if these trees grew right up to it now or if one could still lie down in front of it.

The first time they made love in that field, their blanket flattened the meadowsweet and grasses by the wall. Stella was putting herself through Blaine's Beauty Academy while she worked the perfume counter at Gilchrist's. That day, she'd used the wad of cash to buy equipment for the beauty salon they were opening upstairs from the Phoenix. They'd named it A Cut Above.

They had lain by the wall in a pocket of warmth. Stella might have been holding her breath. They were new with each other. Afterward, Frenchie rolled off her onto his back. He felt he might float right up on the current of his feelings. Yellow heads of grass swayed above him in the vivid sky. Heat of the sun. Clouds. Clouds that didn't look like anything. Cotton maybe.

She sat up. It surprised him that she still wore her slip. He had felt so naked.

"A tornado just got hold of me." She pushed at her tangled hair. "Or maybe an earthquake. Some sort of natural disaster."

He closed his eyes and thought he might be smiling. He heard her light a match and then smelled the smoke of her cigarette.

"I'm not sure I liked it much," she said.

He opened his eyes. She picked at the grass by the blanket's edge. He rolled up onto his elbow and popped one of the cherries left from their picnic into his mouth. He eased her down. Her cigarette, he snuffed out in the dirt.

She watched him. He kissed her. He pushed the cherry into her mouth with his tongue. She took it, laughing in her throat. He took another cherry, and another. She chewed and pushed the pits back into his mouth, laughing.

He spit the pits into his hand. Bits of cherry flesh clung to them. He almost collapsed under the sudden sadness he felt for what he was doing with this woman.

Stella looked him in the eye, steadily. She let her head fall back and said, "I've seen how private you are." She eased herself out from under him. "I can keep my mouth shut."

She bit a cherry and painted him with the fruit, across his chest and down to his navel. She was lingering on his belly when he stopped her. "My wife is home, sick." He had loved his wife, her swift, tense way of moving, the sharp, sweet smell of her—a smell lost to lived-in bed sheets, to antiseptics, to closed rooms.

"I am sorry for her," Stella said. "But for me, that's neither here . . . ," she ran the cherry like a tongue along the inside of his hipbone, "nor there." She licked his other hip with it, lightly, purposefully. "For me, it's pretty simple. So far, there hasn't been anyone like you." She retraced the lines of cherry juice with her tongue. For maybe the first time in his life, he lost all track of who was taking and who was giving.

With his next step, he startled a small bird. In turn, the bird, which hurled itself noisily through the thicket, startled him. The maze of leggy trees limited his view to a few feet at best. He took the hill even more slowly, every joint complaining. At home, he had pictured this trip many times. He'd practiced by going up and down the stairs in his house without holding on to the banister.

He had imagined placing her bone on top of the wall, or tucking it in among the stones, or burying it at the wall's base. He would have kept the last bit of her with him forever except for the misunderstandings and gossip that would come of his being found dead with a piece of human bone in his pocket.

In the leafy riot of greens and yellows, of brilliant patches and leaf-shaped shadows, he dizzied. His shirt caught on branches. Branches slapped back. He couldn't hear traffic anymore because of the sound of his heart working in his ears. He couldn't say which way the road might be, and when a flash of fear took hold of him, he told himself he couldn't get lost as long as he took his time and kept facing uphill.

He found a rock among the tree clumps, a boulder big enough to sit on. He didn't remember it. He tried to picture the clear field with a rock like this, but couldn't quite. His tiredness was a kind of drowning. He could only pull in so much of the balled up air. He tipped to one side, drawn down heavily in this place.

Stella said people would always judge you. It didn't matter how good you were, or how private; judgment couldn't be dodged. "So you might as well live the way that makes the most sense to you."

He remembered kissing her in the back stairwell between the Phoenix and the salon. He cupped her face in his hands and kissed her until they could barely stand. At home, his wife, who had inherited the Phoenix building from her father, watched Mass on television, propped on a three-cornered pillow in her stale bedroom, her syrupy blood slowly gumming up her insides.

He held Stella against the wall and slid her skirt up past the tops of her stockings, so his hand could find her, even knowing that the stairs where he made her moan and buck and fall against him belonged to Martine.

After they opened A Cut Above, he helped Stella fashion an apartment on the top floor, in what had been the attic. The salon struggled, but gradually word of Stella's skills got around. The ladies from Belvidere Hill came to depend on her services. She hired more girls, including June, Kaylene's foster mother, and tiled one whole wall of the salon with mirrors. He told Martine only that he'd rented the space above the luncheonette to a beauty salon. What kind of man did that make him?

Every morning he left Martine and his home, for Stella and the Phoenix. He kept them separate. On those rare occasions when Martine felt strong enough, he'd take her to church, which meant he had to lift her—their eyes not meeting—and carry her wasted body down the stairs. Neither of them said a thing about what she, what they, had come to. He would drive her to church, settle her in a pew, and make sure her walker was in reach—just a man doing what he needed to do.

At the beginning of his marriage, before Martine became ill, he thought he knew everything. She'd attracted him with her swift shifts of feeling and her contradictions. With her, he couldn't quite relax. Dark and quick, she carried an edge of something like happiness. It made him sick with sadness to think of it.

On Sunday afternoons, he'd go to Stella. If they didn't slip out to the hill—where, by then, he'd finished rebuilding the wall—they'd stay in bed in her little apartment, looking down at sleepy Clint's Mart and Sam's Shoe Repair. With Stella, he'd gambled without assessing the stakes.

He asked her once if he ought to leave Martine. She said, "You couldn't possibly do that. How could you?" She spoke with such certainty that later he wondered if she ever wavered. Quietly, he'd climbed the back stairs to the salon and watched her through the glass of the door. She scissored away at some woman's do, offering financial advice and smoking. Stella wore fresh lipstick and had taken care with her own hair. She looked like someone very clear about the sense she'd made of her life. While she worked, she gave pointers to June rolling a perm and asked Kaylene, who leaned on the chair watching, to quit wiggling. If Stella was uncomfortable with any compromises she'd had to make, she didn't show it.

As long as he kept his secrets, no one saw him for what he was but Stella, and she took him, his feelings, his stocky body and rough skin, his long toes, his loneliness—she took him whole and loved him.

In a way, his heart killed Stella. That was how knotted the logic of their bodies had become. He had a heart attack and she died.

He had been at work behind the counter at the Phoenix, as always. The breakfast rush was just petering out. He didn't feel good; that was the truth. Chills, aches, no extra wind. He didn't mention it. How he felt was no one's business.

The cop, Polcari—the big new kid who ate whatever Thibodeau left on his plate—Polcari was the one who said, "Frenchie, you feelin' okay? You don't look so good."

He was fine. Coming down with something, maybe. He felt a little clammy.

Polcari wouldn't drop it. "You got pains anywhere? You want to sit?"

It all happened in minutes.

When Polcari fished in his uniform pockets for a dime for the pay phone, little Kaylene slipped a hand into the cash register to get him what he needed—even while Frenchie was insisting he didn't need an ambulance. He'd had gas pains that hurt worse. The whole thing embarrassed him. Greasy old Thibodeau gave up his stool for him. Maria Sarzana limped behind the counter to pour coffee and flip the cheese sandwich Moriarty was waiting for. If Frenchie'd had more breath, he would have said what a lot of fuss it was over nothing.

Two guys in white rushed in like it was his time for the funny farm. He wanted to joke around and ask them why no straitjacket. One of them measured his pulse and peppered him with questions that everyone answered for him, while the other guy erected a bed on wheels. Frenchie had never felt so useless. He didn't know how he got onto the gurney or who clapped the mask onto his face. He expected the oxygen to smell or taste, but the only sensation was coolness in his nostrils and throat. As they began to move, Stella's hand appeared on his shoulder.

When he saw she meant to accompany him in public, he knew what was happening was real. The Phoenix emptied onto the sidewalk behind them. Stella kept her voice steady, telling him to breathe. Her hand disappeared when they collapsed the gurney. They hoisted him headfirst into the back of the ambulance. He felt colder than he'd ever felt. She pulled herself up and in. Her expression changed. He followed her gaze, twisting enough to see his wife—her coat clutched closed over her nightgown, her bony ankles, purple-blue and bare above her slippers—arranged in the seat next to him. Stella nodded to her, turned her back, and gripped his forearm.

Later, he heard that Polcari had collected Martine from their house around the corner, thinking Frenchie would want her with him. Polcari was just a young buck trying to do the right thing. He hadn't even known about Martine's illness. While they'd strapped Frenchie onto the gurney inside the Phoenix, Polcari had settled Martine, skin and frail bones, into the back of the ambulance.

Before that minute, Martine had not known about Stella. He felt the desperate heat of his wife's eyes on him. The oxygen mask prevented him from speaking. He feared what would come next. Martine had never been one to control her tongue. But it was the voice of an ambulance attendant he heard. Frenchie couldn't make out the words.

Martine hadn't taken her eyes off his face.

Stella ignored whatever the attendant said and, lacing her fingers with Frenchie's, braced herself for the trip. He closed his eyes and heard her telling him to breathe. Then the ambulance attendant spoke louder, "It's the law, lady. Only one can ride with him." The attendant stretched his hand up to help Stella down.

She froze.

"What if we have to resuscitate him, but you're in the way?" He insisted with his hand. "Every second counts here."

Frenchie saw what he needed to do. He wanted his wife kicked out of the ambulance. He tried to speak. The mask muffled his words. He gesticulated with his eyes and fought the straps that held him down.

Stella leaned toward him, smoothing the blanket across his chest, and said, "Hey, can I pinch your toe?" It was a silly thing they said to each other. He sucked oxygen and struggled. She squeezed his foot where it jutted up in the blanket and said, "Meet you there."

Then she accepted the attendant's hand and climbed down to the street. She stepped to the side so they could close the doors, and that was when the oncoming delivery truck hit her. Frenchie mistook the impact for the ambulance doors thudding shut.

∾

What did it matter if he ran out of steam on this cold seat? He had replayed that minute and a half in the back of the ambulance for years. He relived it over and over, trying to make it end some other way. Why hadn't he objected when the ambulance driver strapped him down? Had Stella not understood that he wanted her with him? The thought that she died thinking she came second—that her place with him was provisional—made his breath come short and his fingers go numb. Why hadn't he spelled out to Polcari or someone, anyone, the whole of what Stella meant to him?

June DeLisle, the one who had married and still put up with old Mr. DeLisle's difficult son, settled her big bottom into the chair by his hospital bed and told him what had happened. Little Kaylene skulked behind her, kicking softly at the chair leg, and sucking on her hair. If he had been able, he might have killed poor sweet fat June for the words she spoke.

Afterward, alone, one thought overwhelmed him: he had to see Stella. He tangled himself up trying to pull his clothes on. A nurse found him with his shirt half on and inside out, snot on his upper lip. He was digging at the layers of tape, trying to rip the IV out of the back of his hand. She helped him back to bed with the promise that she would get Rafferty, the funeral director on the phone for him. That someone had witnessed the extent of his weakness still bothered him.

Days went by, and Stella's ashes, most of them, were buried. Then he left the hospital, and weeks were all the same. If only the EMTs had been quicker strapping him to the gurney, he might have reached the ambulance before Polcari fetched Martine, and then Stella could have been the one tucked into the seat by him. He couldn't stop feeling that if he could only shift the way things had happened, a foot to the left, a minute later, even a second later, then the truck would have passed safely and she'd have lived to be sure of her place with him.

Within months, Martine died, which brought him a sickening, slippery sort of relief. Martine left him with the image of her slouched against her pillows, sucking on a lemon lollipop while the woman hired to care for both of them brushed her hair. Martine had never said a word about Stella. She'd sealed the air between them like a vacuum.

The leaves whispered around him. He closed his eyes and tipped his head back. His doctor said his heart was now the size of a soccer ball. He didn't believe it, really. But if that could be true, maybe grief had enlarged it. He watched his blood pulsing on the inside of his eyelids, making meaningless shifting shapes.

What was the point of making gestures no one but he would ever know about? He watched a ladybug walk down a willow branch toward a thick mass of aphids. His stone seat had drained the heat out of him. He could leave the bone balanced here on the branch with the aphids. What would it matter to anyone? He should just go on home.

Stella would hate to see him like this.

He pulled himself off his cold butt. Finding the upslope, he bent willows out of his way. At his back, through the thicket of trees, he knew how Lowell would look this time of year. He sensed the bridges, the mill buildings, their smoke stacks with nothing to do anymore. He imagined Belvidere Hill with its mansions and avenues and, just below it, Ames Street and his house, and, in the shade of Central Street, the squat brick shape of the Phoenix building. The whole city seemed like something from another time. His time.

He pushed ahead. Not a hundred steps on, quite suddenly, the saplings ended. He steadied himself. There was his wall compassing the hill. But the woods, which were supposed to be on the other side, were gone. The hilltop had been completely altered.

Across the wall, a paved road curved past four raw, big-boned houses, each with a three-car garage, a curving blacktop drive, and a sod lawn. The only trees were newly planted landscaping spindles. The houses overwhelmed the hilltop.

He managed the last few steps and rested his hands on the lichen-covered top stones of the wall. They had warmed in the sun, but there was nothing familiar about them. He had probably handled every stone in that wall, but not one of them felt known. He studied the grass growing at his feet, the vines climbing the stones. Nothing about this place felt right. Here, with that bone, he'd intended to tuck his grief away. He'd meant to leave the secrets that mattered here. He had believed that with that gesture, his big, tired heart would judder to a stop.

He fished the bone out of his pocket and closed his hand around it. He shut his eyes tight against the changes in front of him. He might feel some satisfaction if he hurled the thing toward the city, into the tangle of trees. He opened his eyes, turned from the houses, and leaned his back against the wall. He imagined letting the bone go, imagined it arcing, like a little stone, through the air. Maybe it would scrape a leaf or clink against a branch. It might disappear without a sound.

He had meant to honor her.

He opened his hand. What he held there had helped him keep his private sorrow from day to day for years. The pitted, charred bone just fit the curve of his thumb. What had his secrecy ever done, but damage? His heart thudded, almost rocking him where he leaned. He couldn't leave Stella here. She belonged with him now as she always had. He longed still for her to know that—to have known that certainty before she died. He opened his breast pocket and dropped the bone back in. Let them find her bone there. Let them wonder. Let them talk.

By him, on the street side of the wall, an abandoned yellow and orange plastic car, just big enough for a child to sit in, nudged up against the stones. A cat sauntered up one of the new driveways toward a brightly colored playhouse and slide.

Goldenrod, a lone stalk of it, waved next to the street sign that said "Pheasant Circle." The street Kaylene had mentioned. Just beyond the sign, he caught sight of his old white car, parked. And there was Kaylene, leaning against it, watching him. When he least expected her.

How many times in the old days, as he swept the stairwell of the Phoenix, or counted the day's take, thinking he was alone, had he looked up to see her watching him? A skinny, quick little kid not missing a trick—her eyes on him just like this. Kaylene had been there all along. Everything about her—the easy tilt of her shoulders, the openness of her angular face—said she'd always known everything there was to know about him and his secrets.

He looked at the stones of his wall, at the jungle of young trees where the open meadow once sloped toward the Merrimack River. Even his dusty car, where she waited, seemed to glimmer, as if this could be morning in a new land.

Acknowledgments

NOT ONE WORD OF THIS BOOK WOULD HAVE BEEN WRITTEN WITHOUT NINO'S love and encouragement, for which I am happily indebted. The following people also have my gratitude for their support, their smarts, and their incredible generosity: my parents, Peter and Sylvia Winn; my brother, Brad Winn; and my trusted readers, Rebecca T. Godwin, Joan Hutton Landis, David Outerbridge, Cynthia Phoel, Paul Sullivan, Rebecca Winterer, Julia Hanna, Lara J.K. Wilson, Genanne Walsh, Emilie White, Michael DiLeo, and Denny Blodget. For their belief in me and for their magnanimity, I am grateful to Tracy Daugherty, Robert Boswell, Kim Edwards, David Huddle, Marcie Hershman, Margot Livesey, Karen Brennan, CJ Hribal, Susan Neville, Sam Chang, Carole Maso, Pete Turchi, and Ellen Bryant Voigt. For their love and wackiness, thanks to all of my Wally siblings and Amy Grimm, and to Susy Pilgrim Waters. Thank you to Kit Ward, Peter Thomson, Jasmine Beach-Ferrara, and Catherine Sasanov for their time, humor, and guidance. Thanks to Kendall Landis for the summer room in which I learned to write, and to Kathryn Lang for her patient dedication to my stories. I would also like to thank the MacDowell Colony, the Millay Colony, and the Massachusetts Cultural Council for providing time, space, and financial assistance for the creation of *Mrs. Somebody Somebody*.

Mrs. Somebody Somebody

TRACY WINN

A Reader's Guide

An Essay by Tracy Winn

READERS ASK, "WHERE DID THE TITLE STORY OF *MRS. SOMEBODY Somebody* come from?" and I want to satisfy them by saying, "From a blend of memory and imagination." But as rich as the stew of memory and imagination might be, that reply leaves out too much. The story behind "Mrs. Somebody Somebody" began when I was about Stella Lewis's age and living with my best friend—we'll call her Daria.

Daria and I were very different sorts of people, but did almost everything together. She hailed from the South, the youngest in her liberal family; I was from the Northeast, the eldest in my predominantly conservative one. Her awareness of social injustice, racism, sexism, socioeconomic inequality, and discrimination of all kinds was acute. Mine needed development, to say the least. She was figuring out that she was a lesbian, which I didn't understand. She admired Bob Dylan; I swooned over the Beatles. She went for Adrienne Rich, I for Robert Frost. Although my family's alien ways exhausted Daria, compelling her to nap afterward, she would visit them with me every Sunday.

She and I traveled to Europe, dragging everything we owned behind us, missing trains, arguing about the pronunciation of words in languages we weren't qualified to speak. She secured work in the basement of a hotel, sending provisions up to the kitchen in a dumbwaiter. I found myself situated by the sea as an au pair to a vacationing Parisian family. We wrote each other long letters, mine bemoaning lost opportunities with French men, hers about her loneliness and the one other American at the hotel, a boy who played piano and introduced her to cigarettes. When we returned to the United States, we shared friends, books, poetry, music, debate, and an even smaller living space than before. We made each other laugh. I cut her hair for her. She drove me to the doctor's when I was sick. I thought I could maybe help her find a nice boy. If I had been listening, she might have said something to bring me along as, more and more, she defined herself by her sexual orientation.

The next summer, while we were working in different corners of the United States, she quit sharing the details of her life with me. The only explanation she offered came in a note that said, "The beans are still cooking—it's too early to spill them."

Gradually, she stopped returning my phone calls. And then, quietly, moving on with her own life, she removed herself from mine. I felt as though she had died, and the loss changed me as surely as her death would have.

Her disappearance triggered in me a long spate of self-examination, during which I tried to understand how she could leave me behind. I reread all of our letters, replayed scenes between us, dissected interactions, looking for—and finding—my insensitivity and self-centeredness. Signposts of the distance she'd put between us became visible in hindsight. I'd been so focused on what was going on in my life that I hadn't paid enough attention to hers. I hadn't acknowledged or accepted her increasingly political self-definition as a lesbian. In reflection, I learned how much care is required to maintain a deep friendship. I started to pay better attention to people outside myself.

As the years passed, I saw Daria only in dreams. I can't tell you how many scenes of disappointed reconciliation I experienced in my sleep. During this time, I was also learning to write, and I grew to share Eudora Welty's sentiments: "What I do in the writing of any character is to try to enter into the mind, heart and skin of a human being who is not myself. . . . It is the act of a writer's imagination that I set the most high." I began to understand that the loss of my best friend wasn't going to loosen its grip on me until I wrote my way to resolution with it.

The problem was, I couldn't find an appealing context for the story of that friendship. I wanted to set it somewhere young women's lives push up against one another in the way ours had, somewhere one character would be called on to act on her principles just about every minute, and where the other could fail to understand.

More years passed, and I saw Lowell for the first time when accompanying my daughter's middle-school class trip to the Lowell National Historical Park. Shortly afterward, a late-night local news clip about a baby who had fallen into a canal caught my attention. A mill worker on his coffee break dove from the mill's second floor to save the baby. I wondered what sort of person the mill worker might be and what sequence of events led to the baby's fall. Lacking facts, my imagination rushed in.

When it dawned on me that the baby-rescuing mill worker must have been as principled and caring as Daria, I zipped back to Lowell to poke around on my own. The geography (there really are canals) and the architecture intrigued me. Not naturally extroverted, I mostly stayed in my car—a shy voyeur—and drove around looking and looking, a notebook in my lap, a map on the seat. Down by the Merrimack River, I found an old mill building with broken windows and a front door hanging open. Leaves blew across the floors of the big abandoned rooms. People had spent their entire working lives within those walls. I could almost see their stories blowing around with the leaves. Carved in stone over the entrance was HUB HOSIERY.

The factual research for "Mrs. Somebody Somebody" started before Google became a verb. I couldn't unearth much in my local library about hosiery making, although I did discover an awful lot about the inventions of nylon, elastic, and the circular-weave machine. Luckily, I came upon a listing for a book called *The Last Generation* by Mary H. Blewett, available at the Lowell National Historical Park. Ms. Blewett had interviewed the men and women who worked the mills between 1910 and 1960 and compiled their stories as first-person monologues. Her book distilled the working lives of immigrants for whom Lowell's mills were central. Their names alone, from so many different countries, would have made me curious about them. Their stories drew me in. The working people Ms. Blewett's book introduced me to inspired many of the secondary characters in "Mrs. Somebody Somebody."

Feeding my curiosity was the fact that I had married into an Italian family from Holyoke, another mill city in Massachusetts. My in-laws were contemporaries of the subjects of Mary Blewett's book and, like them, centered their lives on family, the Catholic Church, the corner store, and the Italian-American Social Club. I read *The Last Generation* excited to understand my husband's upbringing in the broader context of the immigrant experience in this country.

On my fifth or sixth trip to Lowell, serendipity joined the mix of memory, imagination, and curiosity fueling the story. I stumbled on a heart-stopping exhibition of photographs of life there after the Second World War. The black-and-white stills captured old Chevrolets crossing the Ouellette Bridge, people knocking back Angel's Tits and Tom Collinses at

Harley's Café, the Paramount Theater with its lit marquee, the women's hats (those little dotted veils!), folks dancing on Saturday night at the Colonnade Ballroom to bands with names like Billy High Hat and Holidays, and enjoying picnics in their Sunday best across the river in Pawtucketville. Those photos filled in the details—the salient facts from which fiction steals its authority—and gave me the gumption to believe in Stella Lewis and Lucy Mattsen when they trooped out with the other sweaty workers to share a cigarette on Hub Hosiery's platform a couple of minutes before a baby fell into the canal.

Questions for Discussion

1. Which of the characters in this book do you identify with most? Why? Which characters would you want to spend more time with?

2. A character from one story often reappears in another, as do objects such as the red-striped music box. How do the reappearances of characters and things affect your emotional response and add to the layers of meaning in both the original story and the stories in which the repetition appears?

3. Do you think the author is presenting an optimistic, pessimistic, or realistic view of the world? What specific parts of the stories lead you feel as you do? For example, how do you interpret the last line of the book?

4. In the title story, Stella says "Mrs. Somebody Somebody was exactly who I wanted to be. The way some kids grow up knowing they want to be mayor, want to have their name in the book of history, I wanted to wear a white dress and a ring that said I was taken care of" (page 17). Why do you think Stella cares so much about marriage? What do you think of the shape her life took?

5. Why do you think Charlie stays with Delia? How would you say he changes over the course of the book?

6. If Stella Lewis had ever had the chance to meet Augustus Wetherbee, do you think she would have liked him?

7. What do you think Augustus Wetherbee wants in "Glass Box"?

8. Who would you say is putting doll shoes in and around Kaylene's car, and why?

9. Children in this book find themselves in difficult situations. Franklin wakes to a dinner party in "Smoke." Kaylene tries to keep track of Dawn's money in "Another Way to Make Cleopatra Cry." Izabel Tiago has trouble with a rooster in "Cantogallo," and Helen makes a phone call in "Copper Leaves Waving." Do you consider any of these children heroic?

10. What do you make of the language Kaylene uses to tell her story in "Another Way to Make Cleopatra Cry"? Is she simply a bratty kid with a lip on her?

11. Are the immigrants in "Cantogallo" different from those in "Mrs. Somebody Somebody"? How?

12. Though the stories are independent, there are several themes that link them all. What do you think those themes are?

13. Do you think these stories could have taken place anywhere other than Lowell? Other than the Northeast as a whole? Why?

Louisa Rigali

TRACY WINN EARNED HER M.F.A. FROM THE WARREN WILSON PROGRAM for Writers. She is the recipient of grants from the Massachusetts Cultural Council, the Barbara Deming Memorial Trust, and the Arch and Bruce Brown Foundation, and fellowships from the MacDowell and the Millay colonies. Her stories have appeared in *The New Orleans Review*, *Alaska Quarterly Review*, *Hayden's Ferry Review*, and *Western Humanities Review*, among other venues. She works with Gaining Ground, a local nonprofit farm that gives its produce to local shelters and meal programs. She lives near Boston with her husband and daughter.